You're Kitten Me

Want to mate a wolf? It's easy. Just make him—er, her—howl.

Braden, the second in the national weretiger pride, put Veronica on a plane back to wolf lands for her own protection. With DoPE—the Department of Paraphysical Entities—secretly determined to control shifters through any means necessary, he needed her out of harm's way. Especially since "any means necessary" included the forced mating of the daughters of alphas to humans of DoPE's choice.

But going home didn't keep Veronica safe—DoPE still went after her—so now she's back in Wilden… Back with him. With her so close, her delicious scent calling to him, taunting and teasing him at every turn, he's not sure he can resist the curvaceous, delicious Veronica much longer. Screw it. He can't. He wants her and he'll figure out a way to have her—even if he is a tiger and she's a wolf.

Except DoPE hasn't given up. They have new tricks up their sleeves—deadly ones—and they're resolute to test them on Braden. Can he survive their tactics and keep Veronica safe?

CHAPTER ONE

There could only be one reason for her father's decision. Only one reason he'd lost his mind and ordered Ronnie back to tiger land, er, Wilden. A wolf in a pussy town? Yeah, no.

She stepped closer and laid her hand on his forearm. Her movements were slow and careful so she didn't draw the national wolf alpha's anger, only his attention. "Daddy?"

He swung his amber-eyed gaze to her, fury blazed across his features. She couldn't blame him, not after the previous night.

"What?" he snarled.

The flesh beneath her fingers vibrated with his anger, and the scent rolling off him nearly had her baring her neck in an act of self-preservation. It was only her wolf's strength, and the knowledge he'd never hurt her, that kept her on two feet instead of her knees. Everyone else in the room had dropped to the ground long ago. Colin, the beta, stared at her, his eyes wide and beseeching. She could practically hear his voice in her head.

Submit and shut up already. What the fuck is your problem?

Her problem? Her daddy needed someone to break the cycle before he tore apart half the world with his anger. Okay, not literally half the world, but the man could do some damage.

She ignored his snapping and kept her voice solemn, her face serious as she met his gaze and answered his question. "Crack is whack."

That got her what she wanted. Her father's inner wolf went from furious to confused, his yellow eyes relaxing as he tilted his head to the side and stared at her. Puzzlement was better than being two seconds from killing everyone. With his focus on her, bewilderment replacing rage, the tension in the room deflated to the normal unease that came from being in the alpha's presence.

"What the hell are you talking about?" He still growled, but it was missing the snarl. *Progress*.

"Well, I assume you must be smoking crack if you think I'm heading back to the Wild." The Wild, or the Den, or just Wilden depending who you asked. It was the home of the national tiger alpha and her best friend Zoe. They'd recently celebrated the mating of Ares and Zoe—all four apex shifter groups partying-ish together—and then the wolves had returned to the Lakes. Now he wanted to ship her, a wolf, to kittyville. "Besides, you said you hated the pussies."

And he had. Loudly. Repeatedly. Until her mother had stopped him with a softly whispered hush and a stern glare. Her dad was such a pushover for Mom.

"That was before last night," he spoke through gritted teeth.

Last night. Right.

"Oh, that? That was nothing."

Wrong answer. He returned to being angry, the scent scorching her nose with its strength, and she was pretty sure she heard a whimper from the omega at the back of the room. Damn, they had Theresa in the office and he was *still* raging? Shit.

"Nothing?" Oh, his voice was all calm and crap. This was not going well. "*Nothing?*"

"You see…"

"Colin," he snapped, and the beta pushed to his feet, the order relaxing the hold his alpha held over him.

"Alpha?"

"Remind her of the 'nothing' that happened last night."

Ronnie sighed and rolled her eyes. "Colin, don't bother. Daddy, I know what happened last night, but they didn't succeed, did they?"

"They—" He took a deep breath, and as he released the air, fur slipped free of his pores, decorating him with the gray of his wolf.

She really should shut up before she dug herself deeper, but she'd never been one to do the smart thing. "Look, Daddy…"

"They broke into your home."

"Just a tiny bit." She held up her hand, thumb and forefinger an inch apart.

"Tiny…" This time his breath took on more of a heave, making him sound like a steam train.

She wondered if he was gonna huff and puff and blow her house down. The soldiers last night hadn't, but maybe her daddy could. Though the soldiers had been concerned about picking locks but…

Soldiers. Right. The reason she was being sent away. *Allegedly* being sent away because she wasn't gonna go easily.

Her father dropped his head. His eyes squeezed shut. "Tiny? They were *inside your house*, Veronica!"

Okay, technically they had been, but only part of it. That had to count, right?

Ever since the tiger shifters were revealed—thanks to Zoe's ex-boss—there'd been trouble with the wolf packs, bear clans, and the lion and tiger prides. Someone inside the Department of Paraphysical Entities had decided controlling their kind was better than just registering them.

When five DoPE soldiers made their first attempt to claim a high-ranking shifter female—the national tiger alpha's sister Claire—it'd ended with four dead males. The fifth, well... Unfortunately, he'd successfully pulled the tigress' tail. It bound the feline's soul to the damaged human; the animal's essence twined with the hated man. When she'd left Claire, the young woman looked two steps from death, her normal vivaciousness dimmed. To be forced to mate like that...

The human still clung to life—barely—and the pride waited to see if he'd make the transition to tiger. Then the kitty alpha could kill the male in a legal Challenge, and Claire would be free.

Memories from her own past tried to assault Ronnie, but she shoved them back, pouncing and stomping on them. Her human mind never wanted to think about that time and place—a situation that resembled Claire's so closely. Her wolf had no such desires. The beast was still proud of their actions that day. The way they retaliated when...

She mentally shook her head and really did push that emotional trauma away. She needed to focus on the now, not over ten years ago.

It'd been a busy couple of weeks with the apex shifters. Now, home for less than forty-eight hours and DoPE had tried to snatch Ronnie. Okay, first drug, then snatch. The sedative would have downed a lesser wolf, but Ronnie Barrington wasn't a regular wolf. She was her father's daughter. She was tougher—stronger—than any other female and some of the males.

Knock her out with wolfsbane? Ha! She'd been weaned on the stuff.

Really, she had. Her daddy—God love his twisted soul—had helped her build a tolerance for the drug from the moment she cut her first tooth. It'd been a bitch during her teen years, when her hormones were all funky, and she'd had to deal with PMS and the poison at the same time. But now she could take a licking and keep on ticking.

Her dad's face slowly turned the weird shade of purple that told her she'd kept quiet for too long. Dammit. "They were in the outer courtyard. You know they weren't *really* inside."

"They shot you with a poisoned dart through an open window," he hissed.

She wondered if he was part cat. Which would make *her* part cat and would explain her attraction to a certain tiger back in… She cut off that line of thinking. Nothing could come of remembering the curl of that tiger's hair at his collar. Or the breadth of his shoulders. Or the beauty of him when he shifted. Pure power, pure strength, pure deliciousness in a striped kitty-shaped package. Wait, she wasn't going to think about him.

"The dart only had a little bit of wolfsbane on it." She waved her hand.

"Any is too much. They were trying to knock you out so they could take you and do who knows what to you."

Ronnie swallowed hard, knowing exactly what they'd planned. She was overjoyed that her father now held them captive. Locked up, and away from her, until her father knew everything *they* knew. Then her dad could get rid of them. Hopefully forever.

"You think they'll let us take a shot at her?"

"General wants her howling for someone before the end of the week. If it takes too long, they'll offer her up to anyone on base who's good at following orders."

Howl. The bastards. Wolves could give and take a bite to begin the mate bond, but it wasn't true and complete unless the wolves made each other howl. Anyone could compel a bite, but only one person could lure a howl from a wolf's mouth—their mate. She knew of only one male trying to force a howl from a female and that'd ended... badly.

DoPE wanted her to howl for a human. They had no idea what they would set themselves up for. What they'd unleash if they got their hands on her. But if they succeeded, and she didn't kill the male who'd forced the mating, they'd have control over Ronnie, and by extension, her father. If her mate threatened to hurt her, her daddy would do whatever asked to keep her safe. The perfect way to keep the current hierarchy in place while controlling the players.

"I understand what you're saying, but—"

"No buts."

"No really, I get it, but—"

"What," he growled, "did I just say?"

"Oh!" She was grasping at straws at this point. Going back to Wilden could only end in heartache, no matter what her wolf thought. Her and that tiger? Getting their mat—Er, getting their freak on? Not happening. "What about Mal? You told me I should give him a chance, and you want a tie to the Acton pack."

Her father had been pushing—shoving—her toward Malcolm Acton as a potential mate and she'd resisted at every turn. Her wolf would've liked Mal Acton over for dinner. As in, the bitch wanted to *eat* him for dinner. The she-wolf had definitive issues with weaker males even thinking about dominating her. Deadly ones. Or at least ones involving maiming. It assured her there would be a lot of blood and bathing in it. Ew.

But if spending time with Mal kept her from being run out of her home and forced to face the one male who made her wolf sit up and take notice, she'd keep it under control and date the guy until this all blew over. This was her house. She was staying.

Her human half was stronger than the bitch. Barely. And that control only remained if she stuck to a mostly-vegetarian diet. One thick steak and hello wolfdom.

Her vegetarian tendencies hadn't been a possibility in Wilden. The bitch was a beast at the moment. Damned strong.

Her wolf snarled and scraped its claws against her mind, cutting deeply and voicing its displeasure through pain. Ronnie kept the animal contained, breathing through the jolting ache as she fought to keep her heart rate steady and body relaxed.

The animal had been on edge, waiting for a reason to snatch control and return them to where it believed they were meant to be—Wilden. Wilden with her best friend. Wilden with its quaint town and endless mountains. Wilden with that one tiger who scared the ever-living fuck outta her.

"You're going." Her father wasn't bending.

Okay, bargaining hadn't worked. Ronnie crossed her arms over her chest and returned his glare, ready to prod at his pride. "You want me to believe the national alpha thinks his daughter would be better off with a bunch of tigers?"

Not that she didn't love Zoe to bits, and the chick's mate was nice. But live with tigers? *That specific tiger.* There had to be a way to stay home. She'd be unable to avoid him if they were in the same town.

The wolf told her it didn't want to avoid Braden. That tiger was... yummm...

Stupid wolf.

"I think the media is focused on the tigers and attempting to kidnap you—again—would be pretty fucking stupid with cameras stationed all over the mountain."

Okay, he had a point. Even two weeks after their coming out, reporters still swarmed Wilden, and the PR machine was constantly in motion. Which was amazing, considering the media's short attention span.

The story Zoe spun about DoPE, along with the shots of shifters acting like regular people and playing with their cubs, had public opinion on their side now, but it was close. DoPE's approach was to bitch about their killed "representatives"— ugh, soldiers—as well as the one who'd been *forcibly* mated to a tiger. Not the other way around.

Lying bastards.

"I see your point, but—"

"And they need to witness further cooperation between us all."

"Yeah, I get it, but—"

"Veronica," he said her name with a soft but firm voice. "I need you safe. I can't lead the wolves through this mess and worry about my baby girl at the same time. Do this. For me. Please."

The please deflated her. That right there was why she found her furry ass on a private jet taking her from the majestic Great Lakes to the mountains of Wilden.

Back to *him*.

CHAPTER TWO

Braden smelled her first, the delicate scent blasting him in the face through his SUV's air conditioner. He kept the thing set to recycle interior air instead of drawing it in from outside, but the aroma seemed to sneak in, and his tiger picked up the flavors. Sweet and hot, it called to his inner cat, and the animal perked up, suddenly interested in his surroundings.

The beast had been on strike and refused to come out ever since he'd put *her* on a plane headed for home. Now Veronica was back, and the feline wanted *out*. It wanted to chase and hunt the strawberry scent tinged with a hint of honeysuckle. *Delicious.*

Delicious, and he knew he was fucked. He'd been fine with sending her home. It was dangerous to be around tigers with DoPE on their ass and stirring up shit. Even now, Cadman and by extension, DoPE, proclaimed their own innocence and that all fault laid with the cats.

The agents sent to forcibly mate his alpha's sister were a rogue group, and their actions were not endorsed by the agency. There was no way DoPE would *ever* do something so heinous as to claim *any* shifter without permission.

Cadman even insinuated the tigers attacked his officers without provocation.

So they were rogue, yet still agents who shouldn't be held accountable for their actions? The fucker couldn't decide how to get his ass out of trouble, and it showed. Unfortunately, the media hadn't picked a side yet, and the public remained clueless of the facts. They simply knew there were four dead and one severely injured.

Which meant it had been time to kick Veronica out of Wilden. Somehow Braden had fought the beast and won. He'd even managed to pretend he didn't want to pounce and hide her in his den when he sent her on her way.

It'd been hard as hell—and he wasn't just talking about his dick. His tiger fought him tooth and claw with every step until it'd taken a harshly whispered, "Get your shit together, fucker," from his alpha to wrangle the feline under control.

He flicked a look to Gannon in the backseat and then to Murphy at his side. He hadn't been able to drag Hawke away from Ares's sister Claire—the male was determined to protect her even if she wanted nothing to do with him.

Hawke was convinced he was her mate, but Braden had his doubts. Still, he could respect the young male's dedication. Since he couldn't force Hawke to accompany him, he wanted Daniel. The man's growl and twitchy temper were more welcome than Gannon's smooth teasing or Murphy's light flirting. If either male laid a hand on Veronica, he'd…

He wasn't sure how his tiger would react but it'd be bad.

But Ares wanted Daniel with Zoe for one reason and one alone. If someone came at the alpha fem, Daniel would kill first and never ask questions. If he was given a job—protect Zoe—he'd do it and wouldn't give a damn about whom he took out in the process.

Daniel was a good guy… even if a little unhinged.

Zoe thought he was cute.

Weird.

"We getting out of the car anytime soon, Second?" Murphy interrupted his thoughts, and the mention of his title reminded him why they sat in an SUV on the airstrip. "I don't see the plane, so I assume they pulled into the hangar."

The presence of Veronica's scent confirmed Murphy's words and told Braden she'd already disembarked. This meant she was in the open while the three of them were supposed to guard her and get her back to the Wild in one piece.

"Yup." Braden tugged on the door handle so it could swing open. "Gannon at my side, Murphy at our backs."

They didn't anticipate trouble, not really. Not with the camera crews chasing them everywhere. Even now, there were a few parked at the gates to the strip with cameras tracking 'em.

Not expecting problems didn't mean they weren't prepared, though. They looked like a few casual guys sporting jeans and t-shirts, just heading to the pride's airstrip to pick up a visitor. Beneath their clothes, they each had a gun secured in a holster at their lower backs and another at their ankles. That'd help in a long-range battle but if it became a close fight, well, they had claws and fangs. They'd keep Veronica safe as they moved from the hangar to the SUV and then to the Wild.

He shut the door behind him, and they moved toward the massive open hangar doors.

Braden heard her before he saw her, her laugh flying through the wind and hitting him like a two by four. His tiger roared, anxious to be at Veronica's side. They couldn't protect her if they weren't with her, and they knew she was a target.

Yeah, he heard her, but the longer her joyous laugh continued, the quicker his tiger's jealousy abated. Weird and unexpected. Joyous? Was that what he'd thought? No, it was anything but happy. Now that he listened and cataloged the sound, he quickly realized the chuckle wasn't carefree. It was strained and brittle. Fake. Forced. There was no missing the jagged edge and the unease that filled the tone.

"She's pretty damned happy for a woman who's in danger," Murphy's murmur reached him.

His friend and subordinate didn't hear the difference between the Veronica they were about to see and the one they'd dropped off not two days ago.

Braden did.

"Yeah," he returned, not ready to share her true feelings. If she wanted others to know she was afraid and uncomfortable, she could tell them.

Their trio rounded the corner and he swallowed the snarl that leaped to his lips. There was Veronica, all sassy fire and sex, standing beside her suitcase and chatting up the pilot. She laughed again, and the human stepped forward, his eyes sliding over her curvy form. The gaze lingered on her breasts and then her hips before returning to her face, and Braden fought to restrain his beast. He didn't want anyone else looking at her like they couldn't wait to get her alone and bent over a couch. A growl rose, vibrating in the back of his throat, and he shoved it down. The pride couldn't afford him threatening a non-shifter for getting too close to his...

To Veronica.

When the human moved closer, she stepped back, the smile still in place. He searched her expression, noting the tightness around her eyes and the white-knuckled grip she had on the handle of her suitcase.

It didn't take long for Gannon to catch what Braden saw and concern tinged the male's voice. "Second?"

The murmur caught Veronica's notice, and she swung her attention to them. Her recognition was instant, the taut skin relaxing, and her smile widened into one that was real and no longer forced.

Then her eyes sparkled, those lips twisting into a teasing grin. "Pussies! You finally made it."

He ignored her taunting and swung his attention to the human. The tiger snarled inside his mind, furious this male thought he could encroach on their territory.

Their territory?

Their-fucking-territory, the cat assured him.

Masochistic beast. There was no way they'd get anywhere with Veronica without getting their ass handed to them—by her father. The man wasn't keen on tigers, but he was working toward playing nicely. The Barringtons loved Zoe like a daughter, and Talia Barrington told her mate she wasn't gonna stop now just because she suddenly grew fur.

Talia's words didn't mean the national couple wanted Veronica anywhere near *him*.

Braden didn't stop his approach until he reached the duo. Instead of going to her side, he moved between Veronica and the human. He pushed the male aside with his chest, forcing him to stumble backward, and surprised eyes met his.

He didn't give the man a chance to speak. "Don't you have another flight on your schedule? I thought you were picking up the alpha's cousins from south Florida."

Ares thought flying in some other females—their cousins Claire's age—would help his sister cope with what happened. The male was at wits' end trying to support the young tigress. She stayed alone all the time, hardly speaking, and refusing to talk to their parents on the phone, let alone agree to have them visit.

"I-I-I…" the human stammered. "I filed a revised flight plan and spoke with their mother and told her—"

"You called a member of the national alpha's family and *told* them they couldn't visit Ares as promised? As scheduled?" His cat raged at the disrespect. How dare he—*how dare he*. His tiger saw it as a direct challenge to his alpha, and by extension a challenge to him.

Ares's word was law, and Braden enforced each syllable.

His dominance whipped around him like an invisible cloak. It was a living, breathing part of him that stretched toward the male and demanded obedience. He might be second-in-command to the national tiger alpha, but in his heart, he was all alpha, subordinate to Ares and *only* Ares. He was power personified, strength realized, and feral instinct in the flesh.

"You purposefully delayed a reunion between the national alpha and his family?" Braden took a deep breath, the suffocating wave of dominance spreading farther.

"No one was here, and I-I-I was going to take Ronnie—"

Braden growled, the tiger pushing past his leash and shoving the sound from his lips. Ronnie? To this human? Never. "Miss Barrington."

"I thought I'd take M-m-miss—"

This time it was a snarl, his lips twisting as he bared his fangs at the male. He thought he'd take Veronica somewhere? That Braden would allow such a thing?

Never.

No human—no male—would ever take his female and…

Dammit. She wasn't his.

She is, the cat assured him. Again. Fucking cat. Couldn't it leave well enough alone? He wasn't mate material, and he sure as hell couldn't mate a wolf.

The beast assured him they could.

Fucker.

A soft, delicate hand rested between his shoulder blades, the palm gentle as she stroked him. Veronica. Her scent intensified, the sweetness slipping into his nose, and he didn't sense one ounce of unease or fear from her. Not like what he got from Gannon and Murphy. The males weren't fans of Braden's actions.

If anything, Braden caught a hint of happiness from Veronica. At his arrival? His presence? Or merely because he'd interfered on her behalf?

"You are not taking Miss Barrington anywhere," he assured the pilot. "In fact, you are no longer employed by the national tiger pride. Employee Resources," —tigers refused to call it *human* resources— "will provide you with your final payment tomorrow."

"What?" The pilot stepped closer. "You can't—"

Gannon was first to move, Murphy taking his place at Braden's side as the large tiger pushed the human back. "He can and did. Be happy you're only being fired. If Alpha were here, you'd be bleeding on the street… or worse."

They all knew that wasn't true. Braden was more likely to snap than Ares. It was part of the reason he didn't have his own pride. He tended to have two settings—calm and furious.

When it came to disrespect, there was only one option, and it sure as hell wasn't calm.

The pilot opened his mouth, as if to argue, and Braden growled low, the sound rushing forward once more. No amount of petting kept him quiet. Veronica's touch was only able to do so much.

If they were mated, though… Well, he was sure a mate could soothe him fully.

Mate?

The tiger huffed at him as though he were an idiot.

Braden wasn't dumb, just slow sometimes. Fuck. Mate. He understood the level of his anger now.

"Gannon, get him the fuck out of here. Murphy, call Ares and tell him what's going on, and remind him the bears are in north Florida. We all want to play well with others, so they'll probably let us borrow a plane and a pilot for a little while. Once that's done, both of you meet me at the SUV." He half-turned and grabbed Veronica's hand before she could retreat. The feeling of skin on skin was so much better than her palm on cloth. It had an immediate effect on the cat, stroking its fur with invisible fingers as a wave of calm slipped over him.

Mate, it reminded him. As if he'd forget. He sensed the connection that could form between them. *Could*, but he wasn't sure it would.

Wolves mated during sex, by partners getting each other to let go and howl with pleasure. He'd have to fight to get her to howl, but he knew how to please a woman. He didn't think that would be a problem. It just might take time.

For tigers, though… Tigers shared a bite like many other shifters, but the true mating act came from tugging each other's tails. It sounded so dumb when said out loud, but the truth was anything but frivolous.

It wasn't about fucking. It was about cunning and strength. Tail tugging meant the two tigers fought and were evenly matched. It was a delicate balance between submission and dominance. If one was more powerful than the other... at best, it ended with one tiger giving up after moments and turning its back on a perspective mate. The animal uncaring for the couple's human feelings. A tiger couldn't mate a much weaker feline.

At worst, the ceremony ended in death.

Regardless, the couple had one shot. One. It either happened when they faced off or it didn't, and there were no do-overs. Ever.

How the hell would the huge tiger handle a little wolf mate trying to tug its tail?

Staring into Veronica's pale eyes, watching them shift between blue and amber, he wasn't sure.

And he didn't want to risk finding out and losing her forever.

CHAPTER THREE

Ronnie refused to reveal any outward sign she was relieved by Braden's arrival. It just wasn't happening. She couldn't give her feelings away, not when she wasn't prepared to act on them. Ever. They needed to stick to the whole antagonistic, half-flirting, half-growling relationship they had.

It was safer. *Way* safer, no matter what her inner wolf said.

And it had a lot to say now that they were in the tiger second's presence once more. A. Lot. And it didn't just say things. It howled, it growled, and the stupid animal even whimpered when his hand enveloped hers.

Whimpered. The national wolf alpha's daughter *whimpered*.

Maybe she was drugged. That could be the only reason her wolf reacted to the tiger in such a strong way.

Braden snatched her suitcase. Then they headed toward the massive doors, leaving the other two tigers to do as he ordered. She was happy to escape the oppressive space. She hadn't realized how heavy the human's desire weighed on her until she escaped the aroma. She'd scented it easily, the flavors battering her during the hours it took to travel from the Lakes to the Den. She thought she'd be free once they landed, but somehow they'd arrived early.

Which left her with the human.

The slimy-smelling, leering human. The wolf snarled its objection at his nearness, and she'd battled the animal to keep her fur and fangs at bay. Each time he got closer, it became a fiercer fight.

Braden's grip tightened, and they slowed as they reached the hangar's opening. He paused, peeking around the corner, and then led her to the waiting black SUV. Instead of heading to the passenger doors, they stopped at the front bumper. His scent transformed from one burning with anger and suppressed violence to the smoky edge of concern.

He released her suitcase and tugged her closer, capturing her other hand. "Are you okay?" he murmured.

Ronnie rolled her eyes and plastered a grin in place. "Of course. Tired of waiting, but I'm good, pussy-boy."

If she insulted him, maybe he wouldn't mention her rising terror moments ago.

"Uh-huh." He released one hand and pulled her nearer as he cupped her cheek. "Try again."

"I don't know what you're talking about. I'm exhausted, that's it." She twitched and tried to jerk away from the tender touch, but he changed his hold until he gently gripped the back of her neck.

"You're not gonna tell me what had you scared in there?"

No, she sure as hell wasn't. She wasn't going to reveal the truth about DoPE's little visit to her house. She wouldn't tell anyone about how she panicked and froze when they inched close. "Nope."

"Veronica…"

She'd always hated her name. Until she met Braden and heard it falling from his lips. Now she knew why. The wolf wanted the tiger. She corrected him out of habit anyway. "Ronnie."

"I mean it, *Veronica*. Do I need to go back in there and teach him not to touch what belongs to me?" Her heart picked up at the verbal claiming, but then he snatched the words back. "I mean, the pride."

The action dashed whatever hint of hope sparked with his statement and she ignored her disappointment. She didn't want to mate the tiger, remember?

"No," she couldn't resist touching him and laid her free hand over his heart. His warmth traveled through the thin fabric, and her animal practically purred—even if it was a wolf—with the connection. It enjoyed the contact way too much, especially since they weren't going to do anything about its mately leanings. The wolf actually snorted, practically calling her an idiot. "He only kept me company."

"You were scared."

Sometimes she hated being around shifters who could scent her emotions. Like, a lot. "Fine. I was annoyed, and I was afraid I'd have to kick the pilot's ass if he got handsy. The public is pissy enough. We don't need more bad press." She rolled her eyes and gave him a rueful grin. "Ripping off the guy's arm because he touched me would definitely qualify as bad press."

"Uh-huh." Braden eased backward until he rested against the vehicle's bumper and drew her along with him until barely an inch separated their bodies. "You can tell me the truth."

Ronnie swallowed hard and twitched against his hold once more. "I did."

"You keep lying to yourself then." He released her hand and slipped his arm around her waist, pulling her even closer until her curves aligned with his hard muscles. She should push him away, wrench out of his hold and snarl at him for getting frisky.

But the wolf remembered the last time he'd tugged her this close, the last time he'd whispered in her ear, his lips brushing the shell and then lowering to nuzzle her neck. "*I'll see you next time, baby.*"

She'd tried to snarl and growl at him then, too, but her inner animal hadn't complied. It'd whimpered and whined, wanting to remain in Wilden no matter her father's orders. It enjoyed the quiet breakfasts too much—the time before the rest of the house woke—and it was just her and Braden in the kitchen.

Or the late nights when her best friend, Zoe and her mate, Ares, found their beds and her family retreated to their rooms at the Wilden Inn. When she'd quietly wiggle closer to him and then lean into his side when he lifted his arm for her. They didn't talk, merely snuggled close, and she told herself she allowed it because wolves needed the touch of others. They were pack animals.

Puppy piles were actually a thing.

They'd stay that way, scents and bodies twining in the darkness until it grew late, and then he'd quietly walk her to the inn. There'd only been one time they hadn't followed the same ritual—the night before she'd left. They'd remained on the couch except this time he wasn't passive—neither were. Hands stroked, legs entwined, and mouths… she still remembered the taste of his skin, and those thoughts had her pussy dampening and clenching with need.

Braden ran his nose along the column of her throat and then nipped her, sending a bolt of arousal down her spine. Her clit twitched, silently begging to be stroked, and Ronnie swallowed the whimper that threatened to surface.

"It's good to see you again." His voice rumbled through her.

It was damn good to be seen. And touched. And comforted. The tension she'd carried from the Lakes to the Den slowly ebbed, and she allowed herself to lean into his embrace. She rested her head on his shoulder and breathed deeply, allowing his scent to fill her lungs.

She wrapped her arms around his waist and leaned into him. Relief was a welcome emotion, and for every second she remained in his hold, she tried to convince herself that her comfort with the tiger definitely wasn't because her animal thought of the male as her mate.

At all.

Ever.

He is, the wolf confirmed.

Didn't it remember what happened last time they tried to do the mate thing? Ronnie's human half would never forget.

The beast fell silent, leaving her human mind alone like it had since they'd left Wilden two days ago.

Braden captured her flesh between his teeth and bit down with purpose, the pain forcing a shudder to overtake her form. It piqued the animal's interest once again, the wolf spinning and racing back to the front of her thoughts. It craved his bite, a physical manifestation she belonged to him.

God, would her entire visit be a battle of wills? Human versus animal?

She had a feeling it would.

Ronnie whined and tilted her head to the side, giving the tiger more room. This was what should have happened on the last night. Amidst the soft touches and passionate kisses, he should have bitten her.

He released her and laved a gentle brush of his tongue over the throbbing spot. That gentle touch aroused her further, and she rocked her hips against him, trying to soothe the ache between her thighs. His cock was hard against her hip, proof she still aroused him and he desired her. She writhed, unable to stop herself. His dick twitched and seemed to grow more. They hadn't gone far past kissing, and her hands tingled with the desire to stroke him. She wanted to caress him everywhere, explore each carved muscle with her fingers… with her mouth.

Now. Now would be good.

Except a low cough snuck into her ears, reminding her they weren't alone. Nope, they were outside, in full view of damn near everyone. Sure, the SUV was between them and the road, but that didn't mean a cameraman couldn't find an angle that would capture them.

Great. Just what her father would *love* to see—Ronnie's name in the papers, along with a picture of her wrapped around a pussy.

Ronnie pulled against his hold, intending to step away, but his firm grip held her in place as Braden lifted his head.

"Yeah?" There was no missing the deep growl in his voice. The man's tiger was out in full force.

"Gannon is escorting the pilot off our land and will meet us at the road. We ready to head out?"

Right. The pilot. Gannon. Murphy.

Braden took a deep breath, his chest pressing more firmly against her hardened nipples and then released it slowly. "Yeah, we're ready. You're up front. We'll have Gannon in the back with Veronica."

"Ronnie." Correcting everyone had become a habit.

One, apparently, Braden wanted to fix. He lowered his head until his mouth brushed her ear. "Veronica," he whispered. "You can pretend to be someone different with everyone else, but you're always Veronica to me."

Pretend? She nearly snorted. She wasn't pretending to be anything other than what she was—alpha's daughter and occasionally badass werewolf.

She hadn't been badass the other night. When humans attempted to creep into her home. When they spoke of taking her.

When they talked about forcing a mating on her.

They didn't realize someone had tried once before, and the male was buried deep on pack lands. Dead... at Ronnie's hands.

Chapter Four

No matter his anti-wolf pep talks, his tiger managed to take over. It'd forced him to bring her close to taste her skin, and his cock reacted to her presence. He ached for her, his dick rock hard in an instant as memories of their quiet time together rushed forward. Fuck, he craved her. Even if it was a bad idea, his feline wanted the wolf as his mate.

He'd suppressed his snarl at being interrupted by Murphy—but there was still the matter of their ride back to the den, which meant snuggle time was over.

"Second?" Murphy interrupted once more.

"Yeah, let's go. Stow her bag in the back." He pushed himself to release Veronica and she quickly shuffled out of reach.

He tried to pretend her rapid retreat didn't hurt him. Tried, and failed, but at least he kept his expression clear. He hoped. Braden pushed away from the bumper, ignoring the way his jeans pinched his cock. Fuck, that hurt.

He glared at Murphy when the male smirked and then spun and headed toward the driver's door. Veronica trailed after him, and when the direction of the wind changed, it brought with it an invisible cloud of her scent. The flavors were like a punch to the gut and he nearly groaned aloud. *Damn.* He waited for her to move around him and climb into the SUV. He would have liked to hold her door open, treat her with the care and respect she deserved.

Except the first time he'd done so, she'd given him a glare and a snarl, telling him it was the twenty-first century. Women didn't need men to do things for them.

He didn't tell her the growl made his dick hard. He'd been tempted to hold open the next door they came to just to hear the sound.

He really was a masochist, apparently.

Braden climbed behind the wheel and started the SUV. It took no time to pop it into drive and make a U-turn. They drove toward the large gates, and he did his best to ignore the flashing lights and shouted questions as they passed the two human guards. The men were readily armed with non-lethal weapons, though they did have heavier firepower locked within their small guard shack.

The pride wanted the men to appear approachable yet protective. Or rather, the secondary firm they'd hired to work with Zoe and Darcy, their usual PR rep, wanted the men to appear approachable.

He personally thought safety was more important than looking harmless to the humans. Tigers were fierce predators, not fluffy kittens, no matter how hard they tried to make them appear innocuous.

Yes, little humans, look at our twitchy tails while I rip out your throat for staring at me too long.

Right. He wasn't allowed to do that. He forgot for a second. Especially when an overzealous photographer jogged alongside them, camera raised and constantly snapping shots, the flash nearly blinding him. He gritted his teeth and fought the urge to forcibly remove the male. He didn't think Ares would be happy with him if he drove over a human.

He kept their pace slow while the press continued to surround them, chasing them. His tiger roared its objection at being pursued. Not much he could do about it with his hands tied by public opinion.

He spied Gannon at the corner, glaring at the group that enveloped the SUV. Yeah, he wasn't happy about it, either. He hadn't realized Gannon would be so close to the press nor that the reporters would be so persistent. They'd lost a few over the last hundred yards, but a couple of cameramen were tenacious.

Braden slowed when he drew even with Gannon, not willing to stop completely and give the human men a chance to jump in front of the truck. Without conscious thought, he pushed the unlock button to grant the tiger entrance.

Then things happened quickly, events blurring into one another in a wave of anger, panic and fur.

The moment he pressed the control to unlock the passenger door, he'd known he made a mistake. Not in picking up his pride-mate, but in the way he granted him access to the interior.

That one flick didn't just unlock Gannon's door. It unlocked them all.

Stupid.

The two males on Braden's side and the one on Gannon's took advantage. He wasn't too worried about Gannon; Murphy would get out and assist the tiger. Plus it was a single human male against two shifters.

No, he was concerned about him and Veronica. Because one male slammed his body against Braden's door—keeping him captive—while the other reached for Veronica's door.

Rage overcame him in a rush of fire. It suffused his body, filling him from head to toe as his tiger raced forward. It recognized the need for hands and feet, but all else was in its control. The males attacking their vehicle—and they were attacking—were a threat to their mate. Whether his human mind accepted her or not, the cat had staked its claim and refused to be denied. Veronica was theirs to care for, and these men endangered her.

A ripple of fur sprouted to coat his flesh, fingers aching and then breaking to transition into half-formed claws. His fangs burst from his gums, feline maw reshaping his mouth. His vision changed, sharpening while losing some of the ability to distinguish color.

He didn't need to see in full color to destroy the men who threatened Veronica.

The humans shouted, urging each other to hurry up and grab the bitch.

Veronica's door swung wide, and her snarl reached out to him, urging his cat to come forward even further. Their mate was threatened, scared, and needed them.

The male leaning against the front door was nothing to the tiger. He pulled on the handle and then shoved the piece of metal, slamming it into the body trying to keep it closed. The human stumbled, feet sliding on the pebbled surface before finally falling to his knees. The cat wanted to pounce and rip out the attacker's throat, but he wasn't the one holding Veronica.

Someone else held her captive, one arm around her waist while the other pressed a knife to her neck.

"B-b-back off. Don't come closer." Sweat peppered the stranger's brow, dampening his dark brown hair, and Braden didn't miss the way the blade trembled against Veronica's skin.

His tiger growled low, the sound rolling free of his chest to fill the air. Movement behind the human drew his attention for less than a second—Gannon and Murphy. A short shake of his head had both males freezing in place, but he knew they were just as furious as him. That humans *dared*...

Bushes rustled to his right, reminding him the guy on the ground was intent on escaping. He focused on Murphy and flicked his attention toward the tree line. The tiger took off without a word, soundlessly slipping into the dense forest, Veronica's captor none the wiser.

Braden centered his attention on the male. "Let her go."

He wanted to glance at Veronica and reassure her, but he couldn't stand to see her fear. No, the stinging scent of her terror was enough to have the tiger straining against whatever control he had left over the beast. Looking at her would have the cat slipping his leash entirely.

"No, you guys leave. We just want her."

He flexed his hands, his fingertips burning as the nails lengthened. The cat assured him they were faster than the human. "That's not going to happen. I don't know what you think you're doing, but taking her is not an option."

"You need to back off. I mean it." The male's arm around Veronica's waist tightened, and the blade pressed against her skin even harder. The wind changed direction, and instead of bringing him the sweet hint of her natural flavors, he got the coppery tang of her blood.

She whimpered, and he turned his attention ever so slightly to meet her terror-filled gaze. She was frozen by fear, the emotion immobilizing her muscles, and that enraged him further.

Was she a formidable she-wolf? Yes. But everyone had their demons, and Zoe had told him her best friend had more than a few of her own. Veronica could attack, but if *she* was attacked? His mate—because she could be nothing else—froze with fright.

"I'm going to take care of you," he pushed the words past his tiger's teeth. "Stay calm."

"I'm taking her with me. Not losing out on that money. Let me go or I'll kill her." Panic made the human sweat even more, the liquid trickling down his skin, and the aroma filled Braden's lungs.

"No, you're going to release her, and I promise to make your death as painless as possible. If you refuse, you will scream for days." And Braden would ensure it without hesitation or remorse.

A scream from the forest, high-pitched and bloodcurdling, reached them, only to be immediately silenced. By death or unconsciousness?

He didn't care. It was one less threat to Veronica.

The human trembled, more fear filling him. And the more distress the male felt, the calmer Braden became. His rage transformed from burning hot to ice cold, solidifying and banishing all other emotions. The tiger asserted itself further. His muscles bunched and grew, expanding until they stretched his shirt taut across his chest.

"Let her go or end up like your friend."

"My brother," the human whispered and then turned hard eyes on Braden. "Did you just kill him? Oh god, you things killed my brother. I'm going to—"

He was going to do nothing because Braden read his intent. Braden saw the way the tip of the blade dipped while the man squeezed the handle even tighter. Braden saw the press of the stranger's lips as determination filled him and his eyes brightened with tears.

A glance at Gannon had them working in concert. When Braden rushed forward, his cat assisting him with sudden speed, his friend did the same. Braden's target was Veronica, his paws reaching for her and yanking her from the human's grasp while the other tiger snapped the human's neck in one rough twist. The crack seemed to echo through the air, the sound a final pronouncement of the attacker's death.

Veronica clung to him, silent sobs racking her body as she huddled against his larger frame. Her fingers dug into his shirt and she fisted the material to pull him even closer. He carefully wrapped his arms around her, aware of his strength in this shape and unwilling to harm her.

"I have you," he rumbled, the tiger making the words difficult to say. "Shhh… I have you."

That was when the real world intruded. That was when the reporters, running and invading, shouted their questions and zoomed in on the mess surrounding them.

Zoomed in on the blood.

Zoomed in on the dead.

Zoomed in on Braden's long fangs as he hissed at them.

Their fluffy kitty PR campaign? Yeah, that just died.

CHAPTER FIVE

Ronnie couldn't stop stroking her neck, petting the skin. Even now the wound was healed and completely gone, but she couldn't stop. The pain, the ache, the unending roll of throbbing agony remained fresh in her mind. It'd been different from other wounds she'd experienced in the past and she wondered if there was something weird with the blade. No, it was a hunk of metal like any other. It was her head screwing with her because she'd been such a pussy. Her wolf had assisted with healing her body, but her mind's betrayal lingered.

She'd frozen up. Again. Danger had threatened, males attempting to overpower her, and she'd become a statue. Braden hadn't scolded her for not breaking free of the human's hold. He hadn't said a word, really. Not to her. He'd simply enveloped her in his firm embrace and held her close. A few softly worded orders had the other two men handling what remained of their attackers. While that was managed, Braden urged her into the vehicle, hands never leaving her skin.

He'd cradled her until Gannon and Murphy rejoined them, not letting go until they pulled up to the pride's den. It was only when Zoe appeared and yanked her forward that he finally released her. As she clung to her best friend, trembles overtaking her once more, he'd leaned close.

"I have to speak with Ares. Let Zoe look after you. I'll find you when I'm done."

It was a promise… and a threat? She wasn't sure she wanted to see Braden again—because she was embarrassed. She was a big bad wolf afraid of humans.

Death was a part of shifter life. She'd seen werewolf challenges. Hell, she'd watched her own father rip out the throat of a feral wolf. A snapped human neck was nothing.

The thought sounded horrible, even heartless to some, but it was simply the truth of a violent existence.

Ronnie stroked her skin once more. She missed his touch. Missed his callused fingers scraping her. His expression, as she was pulled away, would have scared a lesser wolf, but she wasn't frightened. Not when she knew the reason for his anger was because she was taken from him.

"How are you doing?" Zoe's murmur drew her back to the present, and she turned her head to meet her best friend's gaze.

The smile was easy to adopt, but the matching emotion was nowhere to be found. She'd fake it 'til she made it. That was the saying, right? "I'm good."

"Uh-huh." The newly turned tigress raised her eyebrows. "Right," she drawled. "Somehow, I doubt that."

Ronnie shrugged and focused on the cup in front of her. Why did people hand out cups of coffee during times of stress? Like a freaked out wolf needed caffeine. *Sure*, that'd make an emotional shifter all better. Man, she was a sarcastic bitch.

She wasn't going to complain about being handed the mug. It gave her something to do with her trembling hands.

She cupped the ceramic, her claw-tipped thumbs scraping the hard surface. "A shifter's life is filled with death, Z. You'll learn that." She snorted. "You *have* learned that."

Zoe had ripped the throat out of a human attempting to harm Ares and Claire not long ago.

"Let's be honest here, Ronnie. This is a little more than everyday violence."

Ronnie swallowed the growl that came with her friend's correction. The wolf saw Zoe's words as a challenge—the woman was basically calling her a liar—and she had to stomp on the animal's gut reaction. Instead, she kept her wide smile, careful not to pull her lips too far back and expose her lengthened fangs. She rolled her eyes for good measure. "Whatever, whoreface. You've been a furball for all of a minute. While you were learning to walk, I was learning to catch bunnies for dinner."

Zoe snorted. "And you ended up getting your nose bitten by Bobby down the street. Bunnies are vicious."

That had her mock glaring. Well, mostly mock. "It's not my fault a rabbit shifter thought it'd be fun to play on pack lands." Ronnie sniffed. "I was protecting my territory."

"The playground was not your territory, and he turned into a bunny because you bit him while he was still human. Then he got you, and you whined like a baby."

"I hate you, and I hate your stupid face." She broke off a piece of her donut and threw it at her best friend. This, at least, pushed away some of the fear still consuming her.

Zoe didn't miss a beat and leaned down to catch the treat in her mouth. "You love me. Don't lie."

"You wish." Ronnie popped a piece past her own lips and latched onto the "love" part of her friend's statement. Anything to change the subject to something a lot less personal. "Speaking of loving, I still think you should have experimented more in college." She waggled her eyebrows. "Our Resident Assistant totally had the hots for you."

Okay, that was personal, but whatever.

"I'm talking about emotions, bitch."

"Oh, there would have been a lot of emotions." Another waggle.

The woman reached across the wide counter and snatched the half-eaten donut out of her hand. Ronnie had to fight the urge to snap at Zoe's fingers. "Our RA did *not* have the hots for me."

A small tendril of *something* slipped into the air. Disappointment? Ronnie's jaw dropped and her eyes opened wide. "Oh my god." She shoved the mug away and leaned across the granite. "Oh. My. God." Now Zoe's embarrassment joined the sliver of emotional pain and Ronnie lowered her voice to a whisper. "You totally tried to get it on with Hottie RA in school, didn't you?"

This was so much better than the fear clinging to her skin like an oily cloak.

Zoe wouldn't meet her gaze. "I don't know what you're talking about."

"Liar, you totally do. I can't believe you didn't say anything!" Ronnie gasped and pressed a hand to her chest. "I'm shocked you kept this from me. I'm mortally *wounded*, even." She narrowed her eyes. "When exactly did you get shot down? Because we spent every weekend together and—"

Zoe stared at her coffee mug, face reddening with every passing beat, and she took a sip. "You know, this is ancient history—"

"Less than ten years!"

"—so I think we should focus on a certain wolf's secrets instead."

"I don't know what you're talking about." It was Ronnie's turn to take a sip of coffee and pretend she was oblivious. No way was she discussing her emotional baggage. Not when the events of the last few hours were still fresh.

"You know, I can't separate many scents with my kitty sniffer, but I know what lust smells like." Zoe grinned. "If you won't talk about what happened today," a hint of sadness filled her best friend's eyes for a moment and then Zoe brushed it aside, "why don't you tell me about getting all hot and stinky for a certain tiger?"

"Stinky? Really?" Ronnie glared. "I'm not saying I have feelings that affect my pink taco, but I'm telling you my lady garden smells like rose petals and rainbows."

Zoe wrinkled her nose. "Seriously? No." She shook her head. "Lady garden? Pink taco? I don't even… Anyway, nothing about your 'lady garden' is rose petals and rainbows." Her friend's eyes suddenly twinkled. "As proved by the aforementioned Bobby because in eleventh grade you farted on him while he was downtow—"

Ronnie didn't think, she just pounced, launching herself across the counter with a growl. "Oh my god, you bitch! You were supposed to take that to the grave!"

Zoe screeched, Ronnie growled, Zoe laughed as they rolled across the kitchen floor and Ronnie chuckled with pure joy. The mug crashed to the ground, shattering and sending coffee spraying into the air. A stool toppled, the donuts went flying (*such a travesty*) and she was pretty sure she broke a nail. She was so telling her daddy about that one. The pussy's ass was grass.

Okay, none of that really mattered because she was laughing and giggling and she managed to tickle Zoe's stomach and pull her hair at the same time while Zoe...

"No touching my goodies! The lady garden only gets one set of non-Ronnie girl hands and that's the wax chick. It doesn't belong to you anymore."

Zoe laughed so hard she actually spit on Ronnie. "You'll always be mine, you crazy bitch."

And they kept rolling until Zoe ended up on top, Ronnie flat on her back, the two of them halfway in the hall.

The low clearing of a throat had them both focusing on the newcomer—Zoe lifting her head while Ronnie tilted hers back. Ronnie's gaze went right to Braden, his amber eyes locking with hers. And Ronnie... melted. Right then, right there, she melted. Her wolf nudged her, pushing forward the fantasies she'd had about Braden. Not just naked ones, either. More like forever ones. She stomped on those thoughts, pounding them before they grew too large. No sense in pretending there was a future between them.

Ever.

Instead of lingering on those ideas, she smiled at Braden. "Hi."

His lips quirked up in a small, teasing smile. "Hi."

"What the hell are you doing?" Ares growled low at Ronnie, which triggered Braden's defensive growl.

Then the two males focused on each other, ignoring the two women. The fangs came out, teeth bared, and they both released long, threatening hisses. The men were apparently more concerned about fang measuring than what she and Zoe were doing on the floor.

With a sigh, she pulled her attention from the angry tigers and looked to Zoe. "Do you think hitting them with a rolled up newspaper would work? Though you guys aren't wolves. Do you have a spray bottle filled with water? Don't cat owners use water for behavioral training? I know you gotta have something, right?"

When Zoe did nothing but cackle and fall to the side, Ronnie huffed and stared up at the two men once more. God, she so needed this. She could shatter a little more later. In private. With no one around to see her turn into a blubbering mess.

For now, she yelled at the two powerful tigers. "Hey! Pussy patrol. Bad kitties."

Neither man gave a damn so she decided to try her hand at hissing. She opened her mouth and bared her fangs, releasing her air in a slow... wheeze. Apparently wolves didn't hiss very well.

Hey, that *did* get their attention.

"What the fuck was that?" Ares wrinkled his nose.

The nose thing was kinda cute, in an 'I don't want to fuck you, but you can still be adorable' way.

"Don't look at her like that." Oh, Braden was back to snarling.

"Excuse me?" Ares's voice was low and tinged with a threat.

Annnd... they were back to hissing at each other.

Ronnie rolled her head to the side and met Zoe's stare once more. "How have you not killed one of them yet?"

Zoe shrugged. "He's packed pretty well in the package department."

She glared at her friend. Ronnie didn't want Zoe thinking about Braden that way. "You better be talking about Ares."

"You better be talking about me," Ares echoed her.

"You better not be thinking about his package," Braden growled.

"Oh my god, no one is thinking about anyone's package, no one is talking about the lack of college experimentation and no one is talking about farting in guys' mouths." Darcy stomped into the kitchen from the other side of the room. "And you know what else no one is talking about?" Steam practically came from the woman's ears. "The dead guys, the unconscious guy, and Claire's mate—the screaming guy in the upstairs guest room."

Ronnie focused on Zoe and tried to keep her voice light. She wasn't ready to think about the three humans. "You guys really did a good job with sound proofing. Good call."

That got her a frustrated growl from Darcy, and the feline even stomped her foot before she spun and fled the room. The second she was gone, Ronnie tilted her head back and met Braden's gaze. "Hi."

They were back where they started once more.

CHAPTER SIX

Braden hunted Veronica through the house, capturing her scent in the kitchen and then following it through the large home. He'd been forced by Ares and Darcy to leave her in Zoe's care, once more, while they continued to deal with the airport mess. Video of the fight, the males' deaths, and the bloodied human Murphy carried from the woods played on a loop on the TV. Wilden was filled with even more media now though they at least stayed off their mountain. The news stations wanted the story but were too frightened to draw nearer to the tigers.

Good. The situation had terrified Veronica, and the last thing he wanted was for her to be fearful again. That shit was unacceptable.

He continued his search, her flavors calling to him as he moved from room to room.

It wasn't until he paused by the back door, peeking through one of the small windows, that he realized he should have stopped here first. Like any other shifter, she loved nature. Trees. The breeze. Connecting with her wolf as she raced through the forest.

Recent events kept her confined to the house, but it looked like she'd sought solitude and comfort on the back porch. With the pride den perched on the mountain, the patio looked over the town below, its lights twinkling and drawing his eyes. They glittered in the night, each glowing dot representing a family snug in their homes.

Snug and safe.

Unlike them.

Oh, they were tucked away, but safety… safety was still something that wavered on a thin blade that separated security and harm. Nothing threatened right that second, but who knew what tomorrow would bring?

Braden scanned the tree line with his gaze, spying Daniel—one of the more unstable sentinels—skulking in the shadows. He'd volunteered for the duty, the promise of vengeance for a female was too much of a temptation for the tiger and knowing Daniel's history, Braden agreed with the assignment.

Daniel, for all his crazy behavior, was extremely protective of females—Veronica included even if she wasn't a tiger. The pride had failed Claire and then Veronica. The pride would not fail a third time.

The sentinels were all ordered to stick close to the den to keep an eye on the home and ensure they remained protected. Chances couldn't be taken. Not after humans dared to attack the national wolf alpha's daughter while under tiger care.

Braden silently turned the doorknob and quietly nudged the door open, careful to remain near noiseless as he stepped onto the porch. He knew Veronica heard him, her head tilting ever so slightly as she caught the sound. He wasn't trying to be undetected. He merely didn't want to break the soothing peace outside.

He approached her, steps soft on the worn wood, and he didn't stop until less than an inch separated them. He stood at her back, letting her warmth sink into him, his tiger absorbing the heat. The animal purred and then nosed him, urging him to close the distance between their bodies.

Not now. Not yet.

So much lingered between them, hovering in that short distance. So many feelings, so many uncertainties and worries. His. Hers. Theirs.

They hadn't really spoken of any of it, but they would. At some point.

The branches creaked, leaves rustling and swaying with the soft breeze. Light reflected off the nearby sentinel's eyes and Braden tipped his head in a wordless dismissal. He didn't want to be left completely—Daniel wouldn't allow it even if Braden had issued the order—but he at least wanted the appearance of privacy.

"Veronica?" He kept his voice low, the night lulling them.

With a soft sigh, she leaned back, resting against him and he reveled in the closeness. It'd been too long since he'd held her close. Okay, it'd only been a few hours, but a few minutes were too long.

"Braden," she whispered his name—an encouragement and plea in one.

He knew that tone, the way her breath hitched and her body shuddered when his name left her lips. He'd heard it enough when she was last in Wilden, when her yearning was voiced in single words and not full sentences. When she'd whimper and whine without begging.

Alpha daughters didn't beg.

Second tigers didn't either.

But they took. They both took—what they wanted, what they desired above all.

Braden wondered if he could take a little more from her. Demand more from his lush mate. She was his and he was hers, and neither had said a word about their situation.

Until now. He wasn't leaving the porch until they spoke about it—until they said something about the situation.

Braden rested his hands on the wide flare of her hips and enjoyed the softness beneath his palms. She was curved and smooth, a perfect contrast to his carved muscles and firm body. Veronica was so unlike others of their kind, pliant where others were hard and muscled. After having his mate beneath his hands, he realized he preferred the lushness to the strength.

"Tell me." Her words were nearly lost in the wind. Nearly, but not quite.

"Tell you what?" He knew what he wanted to talk about. And yet, he wasn't sure if he was ready to face the question of their mating.

"Anything. Everything."

Braden took the chicken's way out and started with the injured male rather than what really filled his heart.

"You know the survivor was flown to the trauma center," he murmured. "Mark couldn't handle caring for all his injuries. The hospital's ICU confirmed receipt of our prisoner and they have him under guard until we can render judgement. He'll face tiger justice."

"Tiger justice?"

Braden leaned down, burying his nose in her hair and took a deep breath. He used her scent to calm him, to push the beast back until it was under control. Even now, remembering the scent of her blood had his fangs threatening to burst free. Only the knowledge that she was safe and whole in his arms kept him from chasing after the male and finishing what Murphy started. He was glad the human still lived, they needed to question him, but the cat was furious at the fact.

The beast wanted to tear into the male, rip him to shreds and then present his mate with the dead body as a gift.

He never said his cat was fully sane where Veronica was concerned.

"Tiger justice," he confirmed and then lifted his head, drawing in one final breath of her fresh scent. He tightened his hold ever so slightly and encouraged her to turn and face him. He didn't speak until their gazes collided. She needed to know him, his tiger's fierceness. "We have to see if he'll survive and then he'll be questioned before he falls beneath my claws for daring to lay his hands on you."

Veronica brought her fingers to his chest and softly stroked him, easing some of his animal's rising fury. Memories of her fear, her utter terror, surged forward with their discussion.

"And you don't think he should suffer wolf justice? That my father…"

Braden couldn't suppress his growl, but he did manage to swallow it before it stained the air. He swallowed hard and stared into Veronica's eyes, meeting her serious gaze with his own. "You know that after we met, after we scented each other, that anyone who touched you would face me. Not your father, not your family, not the wolves." He brushed a few strands of hair behind her ear. "Just me."

Her heart fluttered, the rapid beat forcing a vein in her neck to pulse. The scent of her fear and worry soon followed, and his tiger raged at Braden. It was furious he'd taken their mate from sweet and soft to tense and terrorized.

Veronica licked her lips. "I don't know what you're talking about. Why would you think that?"

"Are you going to make me say it?" Because he would. He'd bare his throat for her when it came to this. Braden wasn't sure what type of future they'd have—could have—but he wouldn't deny she belonged to him.

"Braden, I…"

He released her and cupped her cheeks, ensuring he had her full focus. "You're my mate. It's fucked up and confusing and I don't know what the hell we're gonna do, but you belong to me. Somehow, some way, you're mine."

Her denial was immediate and he admitted it tore at his chest. His tiger whimpered with the rejection.

Braden didn't become the national second by giving up.

"We both feel it."

"No," she whispered.

"Yes." He rubbed her cheek. "We spent hours together. Just you and me. You can't tell me you didn't feel the pull. You can't tell me your wolf didn't mourn when you left."

Her pain stung his nose and he hated that the situation hurt her. "No."

"Yes." He wouldn't let her overlook this, them. "We both ignored it when you were here last, but you came back and my tiger…"

His tiger didn't want to let her go. Ever.

"I don't have a mate, Braden." She jerked back and he let her go, let her retreat a few steps, but didn't allow her to stray far. "I won't have a mate." Her hand sliced through the air and then she crossed her arms over her stomach. "Ever."

Veronica's tone was final, but he saw the agony on her features, saw the wolf peeking through her human eyes and silently begging him to call her on the lie.

So he did.

"Liar."

CHAPTER SEVEN

Liar.

The word echoed in the night, lingering in the air, surrounding her with the accusation.

She was a liar.

She couldn't tell him he was right, though. Because admitting the lie would bring more questions. More memories. More tears.

She was cried out. She had to be. It'd happened over ten years ago. She couldn't cry about that death any longer.

But then her eyes stung and she realized maybe she could cry a little more.

"You can say whatever you like." She blinked, fluttering her lashes as she tried to banish the gathering moisture. "But it doesn't change the fact I won't ever be mated."

Saying she didn't *have* a mate was a mistake. She had one, she was staring at him, after all. She just wasn't going to claim him.

Or allow him to claim her.

It was a recipe for disaster… death.

"Veronica…" There was a deep warning in his tone and it annoyed her wolf.

"Don't *Veronica* me because you're disappointed," she snapped and forced her tongue to work, to push the next words out of her mouth. "We had fun together but—"

Braden growled and stalked forward, lips curled to expose his lengthening fangs. Veronica retreated, shuffling backward in an attempt to put space between them. "Braden—"

"Fun?" he snarled.

She kept backing away, moving faster and farther until she hit the railing at the corner of the house. She was trapped, essentially cornered unless she wanted to vault over the edge. Which, really, Veronica was not a jumping kind of gal when she was on two legs.

Braden towered over her and she clutched the railing as she leaned away from him.

"*Fun?*" he snarled, eyes blazing yellow, and her body responded to his nearness.

Like so many times before, heat pulsed inside her, pussy growing damp as her nipples pebbled into hard nubs within her bra. Her wolf chuffed and nuzzled, assuring they were where they were meant to be—with their mate.

Apparently the animal had selective memory. It didn't recall the last time they'd been in this situation, but Ronnie did. In startling, multi-colored clarity. Though, really, the predominant color was red—blood.

"Braden," she whispered.

"No," he snapped. "It was more than only fun."

"It was…" It was more than fun. So much more.

"Say it. Don't lie. Don't hide. Say it."

"What do you want me to say?" She lifted her hands and shoved, cursing when he didn't budge an inch.

"I want you to say our time together was more than playing around." He bared his fangs and her wolf practically purred in appreciation. Strong mate. Fierce mate. "I want you to say you hated being separated as much as I did." He grabbed her roughly, wrapping his arms around her waist and hauling her closer. She shuddered with the increased contact, pussy tightening and clenching. "I want you to say that above all, I'm your mate."

She wanted to say the words, wanted to admit the truth. But what would he expect if she did? Whatever it was, the price would be too high.

"I," she gritted her teeth and pressed against his chest. She dug her fingers into him, not breaking skin but squeezing his pecs. "Don't have a mate."

She couldn't afford to.

"Veronica."

"Ronnie," she corrected. She always corrected even though she liked being Veronica to him.

Braden abandoned being gentle and instead of hating his new roughness, she reveled in it. She liked it when he fisted her hair, her wolf howled when he tugged and encouraged her to tip her head back. A moan escaped her lips when his tiger's gaze met hers.

When he spoke, his soft voice warred with the fierceness of his expression. "Don't lie," he whispered. "You can lie to your family, you can lie to Zoe, but you can't to me." He spread his fingers across her lower back, the hand in her hair gentling as he went from tugging to cradling her head. "Please, don't lie to me."

Tears stung her eyes once more. She'd never cried so much in her life as when she was around the tiger national pride and Braden. Never.

She couldn't hold his stare, not when she refused to admit the truth. "I don't…" She swallowed hard and her wolf growled, trying to force her to give him the words he desired. Ronnie battled the animal, pushing and shoving. Didn't it remember what happened last time? "I don't have a—"

Braden snarled, cutting off her words, and then he was there—surrounding her, consuming her. He captured her lips in a fierce kiss and she sunk into him. When he lapped at the seam of her lips, she granted him entrance, opening for his questing tongue. His flavors, smoky and sweet as she remembered, burst across her taste buds.

She moaned and leaned into his body, absorbing his heat and drawing his scent into her lungs. He was spicy and hot, the aroma enveloping her in his fragrance. He smelled like sex and coming home, like perfection and destruction in one.

Destruction?

Yes, to her human mind, that's what he represented. Or could represent.

If she accepted him, tried to mate him like wolves…

No. Just… no. Not happening.

He nibbled her lower lip before sliding into her once more, bringing her more of his natural flavors. She returned each caress, each meeting of their tongues, and remembered the last time she'd tasted him. The last time she'd lain with him on the den's couch and felt his firm body along hers.

He was hard in all the right places, muscles honed and carved like his tiger's sleek body. Her fingers had traced the peaks and valleys on his abs, counting each one in turn. They hadn't spoken much in the night, choosing to converse with hands and mouths rather than words.

Veronica wanted to return to that time. To when passion overruled everything.

Braden gripped her hips and lifted her, resting her ass on the porch railing. The board was only six inches across, not nearly wide enough. So she wrapped her legs around his thighs, anchoring herself to him.

It also opened her pussy to him. She was wet and desperate for a single touch, a single caress of his hand along her soaked seam. Instead, he stepped nearer still, fitting his hard, cloth-covered cock against her heat. He rocked his hips, sending that ridge sliding along her aroused flesh and she moaned against his lips. It was something, but not enough. Not nearly.

Ronnie gripped his shoulders, fingers burning as her claws emerged, and she dug them into his flesh. Not enough to pierce, but enough to prick. That was when the scent of his blood joined the flavors of their passion. It was a coppery musk mixed with the smoky sweetness of his innate aroma.

And together, it was delicious—ambrosia.

Heaven.

She moaned against this mouth, swallowing his sounds and then delving past his lips to search for more of those heavenly tastes. He rocked his hips, rubbing gently in a rhythm that drew whimpers from her chest and caused her clit to throb. It twitched and silently begged to be stroked and strummed. She'd come all over his hand, find release as she screamed his name.

His and no others, even if she was afraid to claim him.

Braden growled, the sound vibrating through her, enveloping her in his dominance, and her wolf whimpered with the sound. It wanted to submit, to tilt her head and bare herself for her mate.

But Ronnie wasn't weak. She wasn't a pushover; never driven by instinct again. Instinct drove her long ago and look at how that'd ended.

No. For now, she'd take his passion. She'd take his kisses, his caresses, his lo— She'd take his possession. There was no love, just like there was no mating.

Someday she'd believe that. Someday. But not today.

Braden nibbled her lip once more and then abandoned her mouth, raining kisses along the column of her throat. His lips skimmed her neck, dancing over her sensitized flesh until he reached her shoulder.

There, he bit.

He gathered her skin between his jaws and clenched his teeth. He tightened his mouth further and further until she knew he was on the edge of piercing her, and then he froze, remaining in place just like that.

Pain bombarded her, a steady, throbbing ache that seemed unending. She breathed through each jolt, each rising tide, and released her air with each gentle ebb. She panted and moaned, the ache joining the pleasure she gained from his touch—his heat. The tingles grew at the base of her spine, coalescing into an ever-increasing orb of bliss.

And he wasn't fucking her. He wasn't fucking her or stroking her or lapping at her pussy.

No, he simply bit her shoulder. Bit her and drove her wild with the roll of pain.

Ronnie tried to breathe through each new wave, but the delicious sensation refused to be controlled. She rode that edge, wavering between true pain and unbelievable pleasure.

She rode it until a soft chuff broke the magic of the moment.

They were outside. Outside the pride den. Outside the pride den with who knew how many sentinels lingering outside.

Not smart.

So much for keeping her private business private.

Ronnie gripped Braden's shoulders and gently pressed, encouraging him to release her. Someone had snuck up on them and watched them even now. Shifters weren't shy about nudity and sex, but she didn't want random strangers watching her either.

Another hack, this one louder and closer.

"Braden," she whispered, pushing a little harder.

A loud rumble rolled through him, leaving his chest to vibrate the air with his anger at the interruption. Her pussy clenched, the wolf excited over his defense and unwillingness to be interrupted.

A third feline cough, this one near enough that she felt the air stir from the cat's breath.

"Braden," she hissed and shoved hard, whimpering when his teeth scraped her skin.

"What?" he snarled loudly, baring his teeth and hissing at the tiger who'd approached.

She followed his line of sight but didn't recognize the tiger sitting on the ground nearby. The animal bared its own fangs, curling lips back to expose the inches-long teeth.

The tiger snapped its teeth and jerked its head toward the den, urging them to return to the massive house.

Right. Into the house. Where it was safe.

Into the house. Where Braden had a bed. He'd had a bed before, but hers had been at the Wilden Inn.

What would they do now that they lived under the same roof?

"Fine," he rumbled and stepped away, adjusting his hard cock within his jeans as he moved back. His glare remained on the other male even as he assisted her down from the railing.

When the tiger didn't leave, he snapped once more. "We're going. Get back to patrolling."

The stranger grumbled but retreated, his eyes lingering on her body in obvious appreciation and she glared at him. "That look is creepy when you're shifted."

Like, almost bestiality.

The tiger snorted as if it didn't care and turned away, padding back the way he'd come, tail occasionally twitching.

With a shake of her head, she refocused on Braden and wilted beneath his fierce stare. "I'm taking you inside because it's stupid to be out here after dark, but that doesn't mean this conversation is over."

Ronnie sighed. "Why can't you just give up—give in. Nothing you say will change anything."

"Veronica," his eyes remained hot, but his tone was gentle and his hands were soft when he cradled her hands. "Say it."

"No." Saying the words was the first step to ruin. She snatched her hands back. "And I'm done right now."

"Veron—"

She held up her hand, demanding—begging—silence. "I'm tired and I'm going to bed."

"In my suite."

"In *my* bed."

His eyes softened and it looked like it was his turn to beg. Those eyes, those blazing eyes, now begged. "Even if you won't admit to the connection, you are mine. You're sleeping in my bed."

She glared at him, human mind objecting to his order while her wolf told her to get the fuck over herself. The wolf won. "Fine. I get the shower first."

"We could take a shower together." He wiggled his eyebrows.

Yes. God, yes.

"No." She was constantly telling him no. Would she ever say yes?

Not if it meant losing him forever.

CHAPTER EIGHT

Braden tried not to let his hurt show, tried not to reveal the pain in his heart as he stared at his mate. Now that he'd made the decision to acknowledge her—even if he didn't think he could claim her—he wanted that same recognition. But Veronica was running scared, the fear evident in her gaze, so he let her go with a grin and a wink.

Movement behind her along with a streak of light cutting across the darkness showed that someone stepped onto the porch. The newcomer broke whatever spell they'd weaved around themselves and he swallowed his sigh. First Daniel and now—Braden narrowed his eyes, calling his cat's vision forward—Ares interrupted them.

Veronica glanced over her shoulder, stiffening before she met his stare once again.

"I'll see you inside," she murmured. With that, she skirted around the alpha and disappeared. They both watched her scurry away, Ares turning to him with a raised brow.

Braden shrugged, pretending a nonchalance he didn't feel. "Difference of opinion."

"A difference of opinion that'll annoy Zoe? Because we don't have the time for a cat fight right now and I'm not gonna get kicked out of bed because you were an ass to her best friend and tried to get in her pants."

He definitely wanted in her pants. Forever.

It was Braden's turn to quirk a brow. "What happened to bros before hoes?"

His friend grinned and then that expression blossomed into a full-blown smile. "I met my mate." Ares shook his head. "Nothing comes between my mate and me. Nothing." He shrugged. "You'll understand when you find yours."

Talking with his friend had his cock softening and he tucked his hands in his jean pockets, uncomfortable and unsure as he opened this new conversation. "I, uh…" he hesitated. "I already understand."

Ares tilted his head to the side, cat's eyes staring him down, and Braden stood firm against his alpha's heavy gaze. "Do you now? Who is she?"

He swallowed hard and cursed himself for stumbling over this shit. This wasn't just his alpha. It was his best friend. He wasn't talking to his leader. He was talking to the man who ran with him after their first shift.

Braden stepped closer and dropped his voice, his attention going to the tree line as he spoke. He hoped Daniel was far enough away that he couldn't hear him and if he did, he hoped the male kept his mouth shut. Though, really, the news would be all over soon.

He wasn't sure what the hell they were doing, but he wouldn't go unacknowledged.

"Veronica," he whispered and Ares froze in place.

He wondered if the alpha's heart even beat.

"No."

What the hell was it with people denying him? "Yes."

"But she was here… And you haven't… She was *here* for weeks."

"I know." God, did he know. He'd held himself in check for weeks, knowing their future was bleak, but he couldn't be without Veronica. He'd take her any way he could get her at this point. Even if that meant their mating was half-assed at best.

"Goddamn." Ares shook his head. "How did you two not mate already? Weeks, man. I met Zoe and she hardly left my bed. That was it."

Braden sighed and ran a hand through his hair. "Yeah." He huffed. "Yeah. But she was a human who could become a tiger. A tiger that could pull your tail." Tone grim, he put voice to the reason behind his hesitancy. "What would you have done if she was a small wolf?"

His alpha's eyes widened and he knew the male's thoughts mirrored his own. "Oh, shit."

"Right."

Ares eased toward one of the deck chairs and lowered onto the seat. "Oh, shit. You two…" He took a deep breath and released it slowly. "I don't know that you two would ever have a full mating. Not without…"

Not without her tugging his tail. Mating bites were easily shared. A mate tugging his tail, being strong enough to take that last step and meeting him tooth and claw, was not.

"I know, but that doesn't change the fact she's mine." Braden closed his eyes, imagining their future without that final step. "It doesn't change the fact I'll claim her in any way possible and keep her. I was ready to let her go because of that, you know? I was willing to live without her rather than only have half of her. Now… Now I won't let her go and she wants nothing to do with mating."

Braden gave a rueful chuckle. "She claims she doesn't have a mate."

"Maybe you're wrong?"

"Nah," he closed his eyes and breathed deeply, drawing in her lingering scent. "No, she's mine, just like I'm hers. She just doesn't want to admit it."

"Damn," Ares whispered.

"Yup." Not much else to say.

"That is going to make what's coming up next *really* fucked up."

Braden knew he'd regret it but he asked anyway. "What?"

"We have a situation." Ares grimaced.

"What kind of situation?"

"The one that involves a public hearing with Cadman from DoPE."

Disbelief held him silent for a moment. "Hearing? What the fuck?"

"Our guy inside texted me from his throwaway cell this morning. Cadman will come to the den tomorrow morning to arrest Gannon and Murphy as well as you and Ronnie."

"Why?" He frowned. "What the hell?"

Cadman and DoPE again. Interfering where they didn't belong. He still remembered Veronica's pain when they'd discovered that Cadman and DoPE were behind the attack on Claire. Veronica's father had welcomed Cadman in his home, eaten at their table, hunted with the wolf, and was a friend of the family. Then the tigers came out and Cadman revealed his true colors.

"Why?" Ares sighed and leaned forward, resting his elbows on his knees. "Public opinion. The media didn't protest when we enforced tiger law on our own lands. DoPE didn't push because they haven't decided if the men were on a sanctioned mission or rogue. They still aren't standing firm on that issue.

"At this point, Claire's mate is just that—a mate staying with her family. The other men are classified as trespassers as far as the media is concerned. It's something humans understand from when the other apex shifters came out. Everyone gets that shifters are very territorial. Even more so on the night of a full moon."

"And what do they think about this morning?"

Had it only been this morning?

"You four are responsible for the death of two humans, and the severe injury of a third, on a public road."

Fury rose, rushing forward and consuming him before he had the opportunity to say a word. His tiger was there, slipping into his human body and seizing control of every inch of him. "They held a knife to her throat, Ares. A knife. To her *throat*. To *my mate's* throat."

"No one but you four saw the knife. The video they have is from a distance. The humans present didn't see you rescuing a hostage, they saw three half-shifted tigers kill two men and critically injure a third before loading them all into your SUV and disappearing. We don't even know what happened to the knife." Ares lowered his voice. "Humans are calling for blood and demanding DoPE do something about us."

"Our actions are sanctioned by tiger law, Ares. Public property or not. Tiger law prevails. It's part of our declaration paperwork." He couldn't hold the growl back. It refused to be suppressed.

"I have Zoe already talking to legal." Ares coughed. "As well as calling in an experienced consultant."

"Who?" That growl was still present and some of it broke free. They wanted to arrest him *and* Veronica, along with those under his protection. The cat stretched and pressed against his skin, scraping him from inside out. It ached to be released, to hunt the humans who thought they could put its mate behind bars. "Can they be trusted? I didn't know we added anyone to the payroll."

Ares hesitated. "They're trustworthy and they have a plan. They're already packing and will be on a plane before sunrise. They should be here before Cadman shows up."

"Who?" His alpha still hadn't said.

"He would have come whether this problem arose. Remember that. It would have happened eventually." Nervous tension filled his alpha's voice.

"Who?"

"I'm just saying you'd have to face him at some point."

"You sound like a pussy. Who?"

"I'm saying this as your best friend, not your alpha. I don't sound like a pussy. I sound like a friend trying to help a guy out."

"Fine, as *my friend,* quit pussyfooting around and tell me who?"

Ares sighed. "Walter Barrington."

"Shit." Braden squeezed his eyes shut, tipped his head forward and pinched the bridge of his nose. Walter Barrington. Walter-motherfucking-Barrington. Or rather, alpha of the national wolf pack, aka Veronica's father.

"Pretty much "

"Can't we, I don't know, deny him?" At least until he and Veronica formed a bond the wolf couldn't destroy. Hell, he wasn't above just flat out lying to the wolf. Veronica was unwilling to verbally claim him. Maybe they could keep it a secret...

"We have two choices. We can let him come, and you deal with the bullshit between you while he saves all your asses with whatever trick he has up his sleeve. The other option is to deny him and you four go on the run while we try to untangle it ourselves.

"My tigers won't be arrested. This is non-negotiable." Ares's voice was hard and unbending. "The problem is we've never dealt with the U. S. government in this way. They didn't push with their soldiers and Claire. They're pushing now because those three were just regular citizens. Idiots, but untrained."

"Dammit," he hissed.

"Yeah."

Braden ran a hand through his hair, his frustration and anger growing with every heartbeat. He'd known there would be repercussions, but he hadn't imagined going to jail. Their actions were more than sanctioned by tiger law, and tiger law trumped the human's law. Always. Their inner animals made it too difficult to adhere to the restrictive rules non-shifters lived under. When a shifter was attacked, he or she attacked back. Survival of the fittest and death to the dumbasses.

Some said it wasn't fair. Shifters could sense another's dominance, which allowed them to decide whether to advance or retreat. It was a built-in survival instinct. That was how it'd been explained, in very small words the pencil pushers could understand, that no one—*no one*—could rival a shifter in strength. A human's automatic response when facing a shifter should be to back down.

"What time are we expecting him?"

"I figure by seven. Eight at the latest. I'm going to have Hawke and Daniel pick him up. Gannon and Murphy will remain home. I don't want anyone else leaving pride lands."

He raised his eyebrows in surprise. "Hawke is going to willingly leave Claire's side?"

The male hadn't budged since the tigress was unwillingly mated.

"He doesn't have a choice. I feel for them both, I do, but the good of the pride needs to come first right now. She's safe, she's healthy, and once this settles, *and I get a new pilot*, the cousins will be here."

Braden winced. "Yeah, about that—"

"It doesn't matter. We'll deal with that later. Warn Ronnie about her father, and brace yourself—you're gonna have to tell him you're her mate. It might change his approach. There are laws about tigers and mates."

Yeah, there were, but at the moment Braden was torn between anger at having his hand forced and panic. He was a strong tiger in his own right, but Walter was a national alpha. He had a feeling the wolf edged him out when it came to dominance and strength.

Tomorrow was gonna suck. Tonight... tonight he'd crawl into bed beside her and hold her close, take what comfort he could. There was no telling what was in store for them once the sun rose.

"Fine." It was so not fine, but there was nothing he could do about it. "I'll speak with Veronica. Have someone notify us when he lands."

In the meantime, he'd try to figure out how to save their asses—from Cadman and Walter.

He wasn't sure who was the worse threat.

Fuck that, he knew—Walter.

CHAPTER NINE

Ronnie forced another smile to her lips, fighting to keep the light banter rolling while she made breakfast. She'd crawled from Braden's bed, intent on cooking breakfast and then returning. Food, then more mating discussion.

And it was kinda sorta important considering she'd kinda sorta eavesdropped and discovered her father was coming.

Her father.

And her mate.

Together.

She wasn't sure how that was gonna go.

Because of course her dad remembered that night all those years ago. The tears. The blood. The bruises and deep gouges. She figured he was just as anti-mate as she was.

Maybe. If her mom got ahold of him though... Talia Barrington was all about grandcubs. The more the merrier.

Nothing for it, they were going to have to face the mate-ish problem head on. Hopefully, before the Barringtons showed up on the doorstep.

Her wolf yearned for Braden, whimpered and whined and begged her to go to him. It wanted to bare her neck and beg for his... bite? Yes. His bite. The beast understood her hesitance and worry. It remembered that time all those years ago. The strong hands holding her captive, the bared fangs, the snarled demands…

So, she'd woken with every intention to grab food and go, but instead of finding the room empty, she discovered Claire sitting in the dark, unfocused gaze trained on the brightening sky.

And it'd broken her heart. The young girl was tortured by what'd happened, and Ronnie couldn't blame her. To be violated—betrayed by her tiger—in such a way… It made a woman doubt everything. Men. Her beast. The world.

Ronnie pulled a smoking baking dish from the oven and Claire chuckled, the sound soft, but present. "I don't think those should go on the plate."

Finding the quiet tigress in the kitchen had revised her original plans. Now she cooked for the whole house. Mating discussions with Braden would have to wait. Her wolf wouldn't allow her to walk away from the damaged tiger.

Staring at the blackened mounds of what was supposed to be cinnamon rolls, she knew they shouldn't be offered to the gang. "You're probably right." She met Claire's stare. "How much more flour do we have? Enough for me to try another batch?"

She hoped so. She had a feeling it'd take a lot more since baking wasn't her forte. Eggs and bacon, yes. They were pretty idiot proof. The rest… not so much.

"Maybe?" Claire raised her eyebrows.

"You know," she shook her head and placed the hot pan in the kitchen sink. She'd scrape everything off once it cooled. "This is a lot easier when I have my mom."

"Yeah? She cooks with you?"

Ronnie nodded. "Yeah. She's always there for me, you know? To, like, help me through anything." She grimaced. "Everything."

"Oh." The woman's voice was soft. "Mine... I love her, but she's..." Claire shrugged. "She's an alpha tigress."

She moved to the counter and leaned on the granite, placing her forearms on the smooth surface to support her. "What's that mean?"

"She was just... Tigers aren't pack animals."

"Uh-huh." She nodded, encouraging the woman. Ronnie had a feeling not many just sat with her and listened. Sure, her family was probably well meaning, but many people were all about fixing things instead of just listening.

"We have a pride and an alpha, but tigers don't need the support of others."

"Your kind is solitary in the wild."

"Yeah," she whispered. "The women are fierce protectors, but the mother-child bond is less than others. In the wild they look after their young until they are able to take care of themselves and then the kids sorta get shown to the curb." Claire swallowed hard and her stare shifted to the stone counter. "It's not that she didn't—doesn't—love me. She doesn't know how to be different than how she is."

"That's why she's not here," she whispered and Claire nodded.

The young tigress focused on Ronnie. "She's not a bad person. I don't want you to think that. She called."

"No, sweetheart, no. I get it. We're not just human. We're *other*, too." Ronnie thought about their impending visitors, her father and the cousins Ares called for. "That's why your cousins are coming?"

"Yeah. I wish they wouldn't, but yeah."

"Why not? It really helped me whe—" she swallowed the rest of the words. "It could help you deal with everything."

Claire shook her head. "No, I just…" Tears filled the tigress' eyes. "I need something, and I don't think they can give it to me. They're tigers."

Ronnie knew the feeling well, knew what it felt like to need, but not being able to pinpoint exactly what. She'd only managed to endure her own experience because she'd had her mother. Her mother, who seemed to simply *know*.

Ronnie stretched out her arms and grasped Claire's hands. There was only one place for the young tigress. Wolf land. Specifically, her mother's care. Just like Wilden was called the Den or the Wild, the home of the national wolf alpha had its own name. "I think you should go to the Lakes."

"The wolves?" Claire's disgust was quickly hidden and Ronnie ignored the expression. Before she'd gotten to know the pride, she would have said the same about tigers.

Tigers had tiger cooties to put it mildly.

"Yes," she nodded and opened her mouth to explain only to snap it closed once more. How much could she—would she—explain? How could she tell the young girl about her past when she hadn't even explained it to Braden? She couldn't. "I had some… difficulties… when I first shifted. My father is ready and willing to rip apart anything that threatens me, but my mother." She shook her head. "Talia Barrington is a mama bear, best friend, and fierce wolf alpha fem in one." She gave the girl a small smile. "And the pack den is empty. We're all too old to live at home. She'd appreciate having you around and she can help you heal."

"I… How…"

"I know this pain, Claire." Ronnie squeezed her hands a little tighter, punctuating her words. "*I know.*"

The soft sounds of bare feet on wood reached her ears, the shifting of the house as someone moved around on the second floor alerting them to the fact others were waking.

Claire tugged against Ronnie's grip and she released the tigress, allowing the girl to retreat. "Just… think about it, Claire."

Sadness, pure heartache, consumed her features. "I…" She swallowed hard. "I'll think about it."

Claire looked past Ronnie and stiffened, and Ronnie turned to look for whatever had caused that reaction. Braden stood framed in the doorway, hair sleep rumpled and wrinkles from his pillow creasing his face.

"You should listen to her." Braden tilted his head toward Ronnie and she wasn't sure what she'd done to earn his trust so easily.

The wolf inside her snorted and practically called her an idiot. Duh, she was his mate. Of course he'd automatically believe in her.

"If Veronica says her mother can help you through this, then she can."

"But…" the girl nibbled her lower lip. "A wolf? Ares would never let—"

"Let us deal with Ares," he soothed and padded forward until he stood at Veronica's side.

The urge to lean into him, to wrap her arm around his waist and take comfort, nearly overwhelmed her. No matter how many times she denied him, he was still her mate. Her one. Her other half.

But this wasn't her first time on the mate rodeo, was it?

No.

"If this is really what you want, we'll make it happen," Braden soothed.

"We? You two?" Claire gestured at them, a flick of her finger bouncing between them.

Veronica swallowed hard and her wolf growled at her, demanding she present a united front with Braden. She took a deep breath and took one tiny step to the left, bringing their bodies into contact. She slipped her hand around his waist, encouraging him to drape his arm over her shoulder.

"Us. Braden and I are…" She lifted her attention to him, meeting his gaze, and she didn't let her stare waver. Once she said the words, it was done. Good or bad, right or wrong, it was done. She just prayed they could develop a mating that would leave both of them alive at the end of the day. "We're mates."

Satisfaction blazed in his eyes, the color transitioning to the yellow of his tiger while orange and black fur slipped from his pores.

His attention moved to Claire. "We're mates and we'll stand with you if that's what you want."

Claire's eyes widened. "I hadn't heard… No one told me." The girl's nose twitched and her chest expanded as she drew in air. "You don't scent like mates."

Ronnie winced and opened her mouth to respond, but Braden beat her to it. "Because I have some reservations about the claiming."

Now her eyes really widened. "Oh." Her gaze went to Ronnie. "*Oh*. Yeah, I can see why, then." Claire's gaze softened. "Congratulations and I wish you both luck in whatever you decide."

Ronnie's brow furrowed. Okay, she admitted they hadn't mated because she was hesitant and fearful of the outcome, but to hear that *Braden* had concerns…

"Wait, what?" She pulled away from him and frowned. "What about the claiming? What reservations?"

They really should have talked more about their mating and less about her father's arrival.

But I didn't want to talk about anything mate-related, did I?

Nope, she hadn't. Now she did.

"Uh… You guys look like you have something to talk about, so I'll see you both later." With that, Claire scurried away, leaving them alone in the kitchen.

"What reservations?"

Braden countered, "Why won't you admit to me that we're mates? You can tell Claire, but not me?"

Ronnie pressed her lips together, not ready to delve into the past just yet. Definitely not in the middle of the kitchen with her father's impending arrival.

"Mating is about communication," he pointed out.

She hated that he was right. "I have…" She cleared her throat. She had to give him something. "In the past, I… A male tried to…" She sighed. "It ended badly, Braden."

His eyes glowed with the tiger's presence. "Did some male force—"

"No," her denial was immediate and she stepped closer, running her hands along his arms. "No." *Close, though.* "But it made me wary. It made me not want…"

"To tie yourself to someone." He cupped her cheeks. "When you told Claire that your mother helped you… You went through something—"

"I went through something." And she wanted to leave it at that. "But what are your worries?"

Braden rubbed her cheek with his thumb and she leaned into the touch, reveling in the feel of him. "You know how tigers mate."

Ronnie nodded. She made fun of Zoe enough about it. Tigers bit each other's asses. Er, tugged tails.

"It's hard enough for two tigers to match and go through the ceremony, to tug tails." He leaned down and brushed his lips across hers. "You're a wolf."

His words slowly filtered through her brain, her mind picking them apart until she finally got what he was saying. "I'm a wolf." She tilted her head to the side. "You don't think I'm strong enough to tug your tail."

"Baby…"

"My father is an alpha." Now she was offended. Just because she was worried about her beast's reaction to a mating didn't mean she wasn't any less strong than him.

"I understand, but you're still a wolf."

"The *national* alpha."

"And I'm the national second. I weight eight hundred pounds when shifted. My cat is strong."

She rolled her eyes. "And my wolf isn't?"

"Look, I don't want to fight about this. I want you. I want you more than anyone—anything—I've ever wanted in my life. I will take you however I can get you." Sadness filled his gaze. "Even if you agreed to be my mate, to claim each other, I can't guarantee my tiger would accept your wolf. And we only get one shot at the ceremony. One. If it doesn't happen, you'd be lost to me forever. It's tiger law." He leaned down and pressed his forehead to hers, surrounding her with his scent. "I would rather have you at my side with half a mating rather than not at all. Can you understand that?"

Ronnie closed her eyes. God, yes, she could understand that. She hated that he didn't think she was strong, but she was sure he hated her reluctance and unwillingness just as much. They were torn, at a stalemate, both of them craving the other but not wanting to go further.

"I understand." And it rent her heart in two.

"The question is," he breathed deeply and released the breath slowly, giving her more of his scent. "Will your father? Will your pack?"

She chuckled. "Will the pride?"

"The pride will accept my choice, Ares's decision. But I'm not the national tiger alpha's son. I'm his best friend. If we decide to be together without a full mating, will it hurt your father's rule? Will the wolves accept it?"

Ronnie remembered the well wishes, the heartfelt hugs and puppy piles that'd followed that time all those years ago. The way they'd all embraced her and the pack helped her heal. Would it hurt her dad's rule? No, because every pack member would remember.

"No." She licked her lips, mouth dry as she prayed he didn't ask for an explanation. "No, he'll be fine."

A quick rap of knuckles on wood broke the emotional bubble around them and they both turned their attention to Daniel standing in the kitchen archway. "Hate to interrupt, but," he pointed at Ronnie. "Your father is here." Then his gaze turned to Braden. "And so is Cadman."

Ronnie froze. "Oh shit," she whispered, mind whirling. Her dad was still pissed about Cadman's betrayal. It'd be best if there was a massive tiger-shaped buffer between the wolf and the human. "They arrived together. Now?"

That was about the time a roar split the air and on its heels… a gunshot.

CHAPTER TEN

Walter Barrington—National Werewolf Alpha—had balls of fucking steel.

Half shifted, torn clothes clinging to his expanded body, he stood fearless in front of a half-dozen agents. Agents pointing their guns at him with steady hands. The torn dirt at Walter's feet showed exactly where the bullet from the discharged weapon ended up.

One of the DoPE agents shot at the wolf's feet. The human was a dead man breathing.

Walter remained in place, not in fear, but as a deadly animal waiting to see how his prey would respond. Braden knew the sensation well, the tension in his muscles as he prepared to react, adrenaline pumping in his blood and saliva pooling in his mouth.

One of the men's gazes flicked their way, attention falling to Veronica, and his own beast reacted. His fur pushed free of his pores, chest expanding and growing as the beast pushed forward. He stepped in front of his mate, blocking her from view, and stared the human down. He might not be the national alpha, but he was a strong fucking tiger in his own right.

The wolf might be the first shifter they encountered in the battle, but he wouldn't be the last. That'd be Braden.

Fingers tingling, he let more of the transition push forward. Human nails became tiger claws, blunted teeth became deadly fangs, and tanned skin was replaced by orange and black.

He slowly descended the porch steps. Ares was at the wolf alpha's left so Braden took his right, only stopping when he reached Walter's side. The leader brought his sentinels, those wolves off protecting the females while their alpha faced the humans.

Women and children first. The future of their species always had to be protected. Walter was an alpha and if he fell, the man's beta would take up the mantle of leadership. It was why the inner-circle rarely traveled together.

If Walter's beta couldn't attend, Braden and Ares would take up the slack.

Besides, he didn't think the death of his mate's father would really be a good start to their... whatever the hell their relationship was.

The wolf didn't acknowledge him, the flare of his nostrils the only sign that he knew of Braden's presence. He positioned his body much like the two alphas—hands at his sides with claws exposed while he balanced on the balls of his feet.

Braden looked over the six men who formed a wall between them and Cadman. While the shifters presented a united, fierce front, the human hid behind others.

He was reminded of his father's words. *A leader should lead. To battle. To death. He is always first.*

The positioning made him think Cadman was nothing but a puppet, a voice for someone else's agenda.

Or he was just a pussy.

Either option was equally probable.

"Enough with the bullshit, Cadman." Walter's voice was filled with a deep growl. "Tell your men to put their guns away or I take 'em."

Taking them could be fun. "I call dibs on the two on the right."

That drew everyone's attention, and the wolf snorted before speaking. "You think you can handle 'em, puppy?"

Veronica's heavy sigh reached them. "If you're gonna call him names, you should at least stick to the right species." Of course, his mate had to come forward and stand at his side, hands on her flared hips and the scent of her annoyance wrapped around him. "And yes, I think the *kitten* can take these... people."

He flicked a glance her way and he had to fight his grin. She stood there, still rumpled from his bed with a look of disgust on her features.

Sexy as hell and he knew he was one lucky fucker.

"If Braden is taking the two on the right, I'll grab the three on the left," Ares rumbled into the quiet. "Walter, you get the dumbass that shot at you and Cadman. I figure you have a score or two to settle."

Well, now Braden was pissed he hadn't claimed Cadman too.

Movement at his back had him on alert, but a subtle shift in the wind told him who approached: Gannon, Murphy, and Daniel. At least he could depend on Gannon and Murphy remaining level headed.

"I can't believe you aren't taking this more seriously." Cadman's face reddened. "Walter attacked us the moment we stepped from our vehicles. That's attempted murder."

Ares grunted. "We do or we don't. Shifters don't attempt shit."

It was the truth.

"Fine," the DoPE representative snapped. "Two men are dead and the third is in critical care. There is no denying that fact."

Braden internally winced. Yeah, they'd tried treating him at the den, but he'd needed better help.

"Being a *friend* to shifters," —Walter stuck the verbal knife in— "you know our view on attacks is very cut and dry. Or wet, as the case may be."

"I can't believe you're treating this so flippantly. The four of them broke the law and DoPE will see them punished for it. We can't allow—"

Walter jumped in and it seemed like Ares was happy to let the wolf lead things along. "That's bullshit and you know it, boy."

Cadman glared. "Mister Barr—"

"Alpha," Ronnie growled and stepped forward, which had the men surrounding Cadman stiffening. Braden wanted to growl for an entirely different reason. "Alpha. Barrington."

Mainly because she drew attention to herself. Attention from men holding guns that already showed themselves to be trigger-happy.

The human pressed his lips together in a tight line before speaking again. "Alpha Barrington, you are aware of DoPE's responsibility to not only shifters but also the general public.

When laws are broken, it's up to us to ensure the guilty parties are punished."

The wolf grunted. "Uh-huh."

"As such, these agents," Cadman gestured at the other men. "Will secure the prisoners. I'm sorry to do this, but unfortunately, it's unavoidable."

"Uh-huh. Tell your boys to keep their asses put or they'll lose a limb."

Braden was liking Veronica's father more and more.

"You can't threaten agents of—"

Walter snapped his fingers, digits agile despite the deadly nails tipping them. "You know what? You're right. Not my land." He looked at Ares. "Wanna do the honors and tell them to keep still and shut the fuck up?"

Braden turned his attention to the tiger alpha, smiling when Ares spoke. "Sure, why not. Cadman, keep your men in place or I'll rip off their arms, shove one up their ass, and the other down their throat until the two hands meet in the middle."

Cadman slipped his hand into his jacket and over a dozen growls filled the air, his own included. He froze for a moment, stark fear filling his gaze before he went back to glaring. "I'm getting the arrest warrant."

Braden snorted. "Won't do a damn bit of good."

"I'll have you know—"

"Cadman, quit being a dick." Walter spoke up again, his words a little more understandable and Braden figured the male's fangs had retreated slightly. "Let's lay it all on the table, and do me a favor. You think about lying? Just keep your mouth shut instead. We'll smell the truth either way." He stood tall and crossed his arms over his chest. "Two weeks ago, you sent men onto tiger land, and four of 'em died for it. The fifth is still recovering, but the minute he turns, he'll die by challenge."

"I have no idea—"

"No lying. That'll just piss me off, and the urge to rip off your head is growing by the second. In the past, your slimy ass came into my *house*. You talked to my *family*. If it wouldn't cause problems, I'd kill you and be done with it." Walter growled low and long, and it didn't stop until Talia—his mate—slipped through the crowd. Only her hand on the alpha's shoulder silenced him. "Your plan failed. Now you're pissed and looking for a way to punish us. We can't prove you sent humans after my daughter."

Both sets of humans. The small group that'd tried to enter Veronica's home and then the other set that'd attacked on the road.

"Regardless, you're trying to take advantage of the situation now. You think the tape and public opinion are enough to take away my girl and these men."

"The attack was unprovoked. You saw the tapes yourself. They broke the law." Cadman gritted out.

They hadn't, but the humans thought they had.

"There was a *knife*," Braden spoke up, his words tinged with a hiss and growl. It had Cadman's guards stiffening even further.

"According to you," Cadman glared at him.

"Boys," Walter cut in, shooting Braden a look that told him to shut up. He bristled at the silent order, but Veronica's soft caress on the back of his hand had him staying silent. "Cameras didn't pick up a knife. Fine. Know what your cameras did see? A human male's arm across my baby girl's throat."

"Then *she* should have been the one to retaliate if she felt threatened."

"You know women aren't as strong as our men." The alpha acted like a good old boy, chuckling as if it was a great big joke to expect Veronica to fight a man when that was far from the truth.

Braden had no doubt she was strong and feral in a fight. That thought had his breath catching and he forced himself to remain immobile as tendrils of the truth wrapped around him. He trusted her to be strong, to go toe to toe with someone. He had faith in her. So why didn't he trust her to match his tiger?

"It's why the boys reacted so viciously, you know." Walter laughed again.

"Human laws don't grant anyone the right to use deadly force because a woman gets scared."

Ares's words from the previous night, the mention of Veronica's mate status possibly changing Walter's approach, slipped into his mind.

Braden squeezed Veronica's hand gently, shooting a look that wavered between an apology and a plea. When she gave him a brisk nod, he knew they were on the same page.

"Cadman, if a man's mate is threatened, all bets are off. A stranger, a *human*, touching a shifter's mate is pretty much guaranteed a hurting for laying a hand on her. They put their hands on Veronica and my men reacted accordingly. There was a threat to the national second's mate." He held Cadman's stare. "I have a right to protect my mate."

Walter stiffened at the first mention of mates and the wolf's gaze slowly panned from the gathered humans to gradually center on Braden.

Braden was damned proud of himself for not flinching. Not when the wolf captured his gaze, nor when a massive, claw-tipped paw came to rest on his shoulder.

Then the alpha flashed him a toothy smile, baring his fangs, and gifted that grin to the humans. As a group, they stilled.

"Plain fact is, Braden and his men not only protected my daughter, but he defended his mate. Those boys were paid—by their own admission—to get my baby girl. I'm just glad her mate was there to take care of things. Otherwise, I woulda had to go hunting. Bit disappointing, though…" Between one heartbeat and the next, Walter's fangs were full length. "You know how I like a good hunt."

Cadman should, Braden had heard stories of the two men entering the forest together. Walter on four feet, and Cadman with a gun.

"Mates." The DoPE agent swallowed hard. "I'll have to contact legal. I don't believe tigers have a law—"

Walter interrupted. "Even if tigers don't, wolves do, and you know it. She's a wolf. He's her mate." The wolf released him and stood tall, the rest of their group taking cues from him and tensing as well. "This meeting is done, and the pack and pride will release a joint statement expressing our regrets at such a loss."

"Intelligence never mentioned your daughter was mated."

Ronnie froze, and he knew she felt his same shock at his words. "Intelligence?"

Cadman smiled at his mate, a tinge of evil filling the expression and Braden resisted the urge to tear into the male. "It's been reported you're still single."

"And those reports are wrong," Walter inserted smoothly. "They're mates. The party is tonight, and the papers will have pictures of the happy couple by morning along with our condolences." Walter held out his hand. "Sorry they failed, Cadman. Maybe they'll have better luck next time."

The human took a deep breath, and his smarmy fake smile was back in place. "You're wrong about our agency and my people. The last thing we ever want is to harm shifters. You know it's in our mission statement." Cadman's gaze turned to them and Braden took a step to the right, cutting off the male's vision. He wouldn't look at Veronica. Ever. The human's gaze flickered with frustration but soon smoothed out.

"I'm happy to hear of the new mating. I'm sorry this unpleasantness marred such a joyous time. Hopefully, this little misunderstanding won't cause problems in the future. I believe it'd be a good idea to pool our resources and investigate who threatened Ronnie both in the Lakes and here in Wilden." Cadman looked to Ares. "Is there someone local I can coordinate with?"

He sensed Ares's struggles with his inner beast before he spoke. They all knew Cadman was a snake and had discussed this eventuality. If the human extended an olive branch, they'd place nice. He was a dangerous enemy to have, and even if they knew he was guilty, they'd wait until he hanged himself.

Let him get caught in his own web. Hopefully in public.

Ares's teeth were still clenched. "Of course. I'll have one of my men contact your office to discuss the prisoner still in ICU. Right now we need to prepare for a party. So while it's been great to see you…"

"Yes, we have other appointments. I'll look for that call in the coming days." Cadman tilted his head. "Alpha Jones, Alpha Barrington, Ronnie, it was wonderful seeing you."

Right.

They remained silent as the humans piled into their vehicles, two large SUVs filling with the agents and then turning until they were headed down the driveway. They slowly followed the curve until they were hidden from view by trees.

Everyone remained silent for one minute, and then two, but then the world exploded around them.

Verbally anyway.

"Mating party?" Braden felt the need to ask the obvious question.

"*Mating party?*" Veronica sounded more appalled than him.

"You're mated?" Walter's voice was deadly calm, bringing with it a thick silence.

That was followed by a high-pitched squeal and a dark haired woman rushing forward. Braden got a quick impression of features that resembled his mate and then Veronica was swallowed by the celebrating woman. "My baby is mated!"

That effectively blasted away any remaining tenseness and everyone scattered, leaving Braden with Walter.

The wolf sized him up, gaze traveling from his feet and then moving higher until their gazes clashed.

Normally, Braden wasn't one to be cowed by any male. He was the national second, a fierce and deadly tiger. He'd defended his pride and would do so for many years to come. He wasn't a pussy.

Except, apparently, when it came to Veronica's father.

CHAPTER ELEVEN

They forgot Braden was a tiger. Or rather, they didn't fully comprehend a tiger's strengths and abilities. Conceptually, they were probably aware of his species, but they didn't recall what that meant.

So when they whisked Veronica off to a second floor guest room to discuss the mating and make plans—establish a "command central"—he'd let her go. He wouldn't be away from her for long. A puny ten-foot leap was nothing for a tiger.

For now he'd bide his time… and stay the hell away from Walter Barrington. He'd already spent enough time with the male, locked away with Ares and a few of their sentinels. They went over contingency plans, how to keep the tigers and wolves safe during the party and the coming days. Veronica's parents, apparently, weren't leaving just yet, and Walter was concerned about his baby girl once he left.

Braden wasn't letting anything else happen to her. She'd endured enough in the few moments she was held by the human and he didn't want her to feel fear again.

Of course, to protect her, she actually had to be with him.

Which she wasn't.

Still.

No matter. He simply relaxed against the couch, the leather cradling him as he sipped his beer. The liquid went down smoothly, but he hardly tasted the drink. He was too preoccupied by the goings on in the house. With his seat positioned within sight of the stairway, he kept his head pointed toward the television, but his gaze kept track of who came and went on the stairs. He watched one of Veronica's sisters—Violet—go up, then race down. Then there were the Jones cousins giggling and running. Talia Barrington seemed to float everywhere she went, a picture of calm.

He just had to wait for the right mix of people to be upstairs. Primarily, women he could easily chase off so he could have time alone with his mate.

They needed to, he gulped, talk.

The slam of a door preceded the soft pad of bare feet on the carpeted steps and then Violet and Talia came into view. The two women spoke softly, pausing at the bottom of the stairs when Talia hugged her daughter close. If he wasn't so consumed with the need to get to Veronica, he'd find the scene touching.

As it was, he saw the women as adversaries and he didn't have time to get gooey about those two. He had a plan—a goal— and those two were part of the blockade.

Their murmurs grew faint, both of them heading toward the kitchen. The soft clink of silverware and plates told him they were preparing lunch. They wouldn't be heading back upstairs anytime soon.

No time like the present.

He slowly stood, quietly placing his empty bottle on the end table as he headed toward the front door. This was where their plan to keep the groom away fell to shit. Talia Barrington thought like a wolf and wolves couldn't leap from the ground to the second-floor balcony.

Braden could without breaking a sweat.

He eased from the house and slowly made his way toward the far corner. The double doors leading from the bedroom to the balcony were wide open and soft tinkling laughter reached him.

Veronica's laughter. And it was a true laugh, not like the tittering she'd given the pilot. The pilot who'd flirted and made her uncomfortable.

The thought had him growling and he quickly swallowed the sound. He—and the tiger—needed to focus on their goal and not the past.

Tiger told them they could kill the human pilot to take care of the past and then they could look to the future.

Braden admitted the idea had merit. At least until his animal pushed against its bindings, stretching the mental chains and scouring his mind. It wanted out to do as it desired.

He reminded the cat they couldn't have a mate or mating party if they went off to hunt the human. Grumbling, the tiger agreed and decided they could do that tomorrow.

Bloodthirsty beast.

The animal remained quiet, not denying the accusation.

Braden stopped near the balcony, eyeing the distance and staring at the railing. Yeah, it'd take his weight. He hoped. Otherwise he'd owe Ares a new balcony and have a few new bruises from when he fell on his ass.

No matter what, he was getting up there and he was gonna have a few minutes alone with his mate. Period.

He paused, took a deep breath and released it slowly before repeating the action. He didn't want the whole beast busting free. He just needed a hint of the cat's strength. With another soothing inhale and exhale, he tightened his body, muscles tensing in preparation of his jump. He bent his legs slightly while he fisted his hands. When he relaxed his fingers, claws tipped the digits.

From there it took one solid leap and his hands were on the rail. Bringing his knees up, he placed his feet on the edge of the balcony. A quick push and he vaulted up and over until he stood just outside the double doors that led to his mate.

He took a moment to watch her, to see her wide smile and the joy in her eyes. She looked… happy. Joyful? Excited?

Yes to both. At least he thought so. But before they went forward with anything, he'd *know* so. He wouldn't have her pushed and prodded into anything. She'd come to him willingly or he'd fight tooth and nail until she was ready.

The wind picked up, swirling into the room and then curling outward toward him, sending her scent spiraling around his body. He hardened immediately, the sweetness of her flavors bringing his arousal rushing forward. His dick throbbed, pulsing with need, and he fought his body's desperation for her. The cat snarled and growled, hating that he withheld his instinctual craving for his mate.

She'd agreed to their mating already, hadn't objected to his announcement in the front yard and even told her father it was happening. *She agreed.*

That should be enough for Braden's human mind.

It wasn't.

Which was why he padded forward and stepped into the room. Why, when the alpha's twin cousins—he couldn't tell them apart—gave him surprised glances and attempted to stop him, he silenced them with a snarl.

"You're not supposed to be in here." Twin A glared at him.

Twin B's voice was softer, but no less annoyed. "It's bad luck to see—"

"No," he rasped, gaze locked on Veronica. Her wide eyes met his and then those orbs darkened with a sensual heat that was familiar to him. He took a calming breath and released it slowly before focusing on the cousins. "No, I'm not leaving. I need to talk to Veronica before anything else happens and I'm going to do that." Both women opened their mouths to object, but he cut them off before they said a word. "Alone. No wolves, no tigers. Just us. Now."

"Ares will—"

"Talia said—"

Twin A then B. Or Twin B then A?

"Out." He snarled, not caring that he spoke harshly to his alpha's family. God love 'em, but he needed space.

Both women sniffed with annoyance but rose from the bed, anger blazing in their eyes.

"Ares will hear about this."

"Just see if he doesn't."

He stopped trying to tell them apart and merely watched them leave. The second they whisked through the door, he shut it quietly behind them and turned the lock with a twist of his wrist. He strode to the double doors and did the same, securing them in the space.

No interruptions.

"Braden? What's going on?" Concern marred her features, her eyebrows pinched.

He huffed. No easy way to say it or lead her into the conversation, so he simply laid it out. "Do you want to mate me or are you just doing this to save our asses? Because I want you, but not like that—like this."

Veronica rose from her seat, eyes wide with surprise. "Of course I…"

And that's when he knew. That's when he saw a sadness and unease fill her expression. As her words trailed off, he saw the truth.

"No," he rasped the word. She wasn't ready. Was he?

The tiger assured him they were. The tail tugging was still iffy, but they'd take Veronica any way they could even if that meant a half mating. With her at his side, the rest didn't matter.

"No, you're doing it to save us and while I appreciate it— Gannon and Murphy appreciate it—we don't need to tie our lives together." Her face paled and she took a step back, putting a hint more space between them. "I want you more than life itself, but I won't have you that way. Forced. Without a choice. Not ever."

Her pain seared his nose and he knew his own swirled in the air as well, clouding the room with their shared heartache.

"It's not that I don't want you…" her voice was soft and he snorted.

Right.

"I don't—didn't—want *anyone*, Braden."

Didn't was past tense. Maybe they'd be okay, then.

He ran a hand through his hair, fighting the frustration and his cat's impatience. The animal urged him to snatch her and carry her into the forest. Find a nice quiet place and show her why he'd make a good mate. He could be what she needed, dammit.

He huffed and strode toward her, unable to have a conversation about mating without his hands on her skin. The tiger craved her and demanded the connection. If they weren't mating her, they'd touch her. She liked his touch. She just didn't want his bite or... anything else.

The knowledge hurt more than it should.

He wrapped his arms around her waist and tugged her close, resting his chin atop her head when she laid her cheek on his chest. "I'll talk with your father and Ares. We'll figure it out. We can turn this into a big party instead of a mating party. I'll fix it."

Braden tried not to let his disappointment fill his voice but he was sure he failed.

"No, I..." She withdrew, shaking her head. "I..." she sighed. "I need to talk about it. I need to explain. I need to..." Tears blurred her eyes, moisture gathering on her lashes and then one slipped down her cheek. "I," she swallowed hard. "I thought I had a mate once." He suppressed his objection. Barely. "I thought I had a mate and then I..." Another tear snaked down her cheek. "I killed him."

CHAPTER TWELVE

There, Ronnie said the words. They were out and now he knew and now… he could do whatever he was gonna do.

She expected him to walk away. Who wanted a mate who'd killed the last man who'd tried to get frisky with her?

Braden apparently.

He didn't let her go when she pulled away. In fact, he held her tighter, hugging her firmly before sweeping her into his arms and carrying her to a nearby chair. She didn't fight him when he lowered to the seat nor when he rested her in his lap.

He held her tenderly, but she sensed the underlying emotions coursing through him. He was frustrated, angry, tense, and living on the edge of rage. She stroked his chest, fingers sliding over his cloth-covered skin with gentle strokes.

"Tell me," he gritted out.

"Braden." She sighed.

He pressed a kiss to her temple and murmured against her skin. "Tell me. I need to know because I *am* your mate. I will battle anyone who tries to force you to do something you don't want to do, but I can't fight for you if I don't know what I'm fighting." He nuzzled her neck and she breathed in his heated, smoky scent. "Tell me."

"I…" she whispered and licked her lips, trying to decide where to start. Trying to decide how best to explain without destroying herself with the memories. And that's when she realized there was no way she'd come out on the other side of this whole. It'd be painful, draining, and she prayed he would still be there when she was done.

"Once upon a time, in the land surrounding the Great Lakes," she cleared her throat and blinked back the tears that kept coming, "there was a young girl—wolf. And there was a young boy—another wolf. And they were in love. Or at least, that's what she thought it was."

She felt rather than heard Braden's answering growl and she rubbed her cheek on his chest, soothing him. No matter what she revealed, no matter her worries, he was still her mate. Hers.

Ronnie let her mind drift back a little more. She remembered her first date. And her second. Then her third. Her father hated she had a boyfriend, but they'd been *in love*. Her mother told her dad to back off and let Ronnie make her own mistakes.

What a fucking mistake.

"He had blond hair, bright blue eyes, and he always had a smile for me." The picture-perfect boy next door. "We were always together. The pack house, runs, breakfast on the way to school, and half the time he had dinner with us." She grinned remembering her father's reaction to Michael. "Daddy hated him." She tilted her head back and met Braden's stare. "I mean, *hated*. If he could have legally taken Michael out and buried him in the backyard, he would have." Ronnie took care of the problem for him, though. "Mom made him play nice and wouldn't let him run Michael off."

"You know that no matter what, I won't be run off either, right? You're mine. Whatever happens, you're mine."

Ronnie nodded. She did know.

She also knew she needed to keep going, keep telling the story before she chickened out.

"So, that boy and that girl dated all through senior year. They fooled around a lot, but wolf law is pretty damned specific. Even if a couple *thinks* they might be mates, there's no mating going on before they turned eighteen. Things change for a shifter when they reach that age. Or at least, wolves do." Braden nodded, confirming tigers were the same. "Well, that boy and that girl stayed together through graduation and that girl was *convinced* the boy was her mate. Hand to God, no fooling, he was *hers*."

Damn, but she'd loved him. Soul-deep and forever ever kind of love. At least, that's what she'd thought then. She knew better now.

Tears stung her eyes and blurred her vision, and she brushed away the first that trailed down her cheek. She wasn't sure why she bothered. She knew more were right behind.

Braden's strength surrounded her, bolstering her, and she knew she'd need it to get through the rest.

Ronnie sniffled. "Then she turned eighteen, and at her first full moon, everything changed. The world smelled different, the sounds were louder, and the colors were just *more*."

"It's overwhelming," he murmured and she nodded.

"It is. And that's when she realized the boy she loved wasn't the male her wolf wanted." She drew in a shaky breath and released it slowly. "At first, she fought the animal. She told it to get in line because her human half wanted Michael."

Ronnie closed her eyes, trying to view her memories without emotions clogging her vision. But yeah, that wasn't gonna work. Her wolf wouldn't let her forget. Not ever. It shoved the rest of her poisonous history into the light and demanded she look at what not trusting the beast had caused.

"What happened?" Braden's voice was soft, encouraging but not demanding.

"I was supposed to go to college." She ruefully grinned. "Daddy refused to let me attend community college. His daughter was going to a fancy school. *The alpha has spoken.*" She mimicked her father and got an answering chuckle from her mate. "But I wanted to stay with Michael." She sighed. "The only way to defy him was to mate Michael."

"Alphas can't separate mates." He squeezed her with a gentle hug though she sensed his roiling emotions.

"*No one* can forcibly separate mates. Leaving them behind voluntarily is one thing. Tearing them apart is another." She closed her eyes, remembering the midnight picnic, the bright moon, the soft tinkle of the flowing river and the rustling trees. "So that was the plan."

"Did Walter try to stop you?"

Ronnie snorted. "If that'd been the case, Michael would have lived, at least." She huffed. "God, this is the hard part." She stared down at her hands, the deep lines of her palms and delicate fingers hiding her wolf's claws. "We're predators. We know what blood looks like on fur. What it tastes like when we pounce on a deer." She made a fist and then relaxed her fingers. "It's scary as hell when you find your hands dripping with a person's blood, and your wolf is begging for more. Not an animal's, but a person's—a man's."

They'd been nude together before, exploring each other's bodies and going as far as they could without crossing the final line, the final mark in the sand.

"It was our first time, you know. He was nervous. I was nervous but excited. We were going to show my dad that his word wasn't law. I was an adult, and he was my mate, and that was that." She lifted her attention to meet Braden's gaze. "But he wasn't, you are, and I get that now. I understand the difference since I've met you, but those minutes will haunt me forever. They'll make me doubt the wolf and myself." Ronnie shook her head. "I'm beating around the bush.

She swallowed hard and continued. "Like tigers, part of a wolf's mating ritual is the bite. But also like tigers, there's more, a way for the animals to prove the two belong together. For wolves, our partner has to make us howl during sex. It's the ultimate show of trust and acceptance, you know? It binds their souls, much like…"

"Pulling a tail," Braden whispered.

"Yeah. And Michael… My wolf…" She nibbled her lower lip. "He wasn't my mate, and it became clear as soon as we got naked and started…" The moment he slipped inside her, pinning her to the ground with his bulk. Except her wolf knew he wasn't strong enough to keep her captured. Even as seconds passed, as he tried to get her body to respond and she wrapped her legs around his waist, the beast refused to accept him. "And he got angry, so damned angry my wolf wouldn't… he couldn't make me…"

Trembles overtook her, the same ones that always assaulted her when she remembered. He held her tighter, imbuing her with his strength and that allowed her to continue. "And when it became obvious it wasn't going to happen, he just lost it. He said if he couldn't get me to howl in pleasure, it'd be in pain. That maybe the alpha's bitch daughter got off on that." Ronnie's fingers stroked the base of her throat. "He said he hadn't spent so much time courting me to be denied now. So when he tried to strangle me…" She tried to distance herself from the past. "So that boy tried to strangle that girl, and that girl's wolf objected. Loudly. Viciously."

"He wasn't successful." His tone was a grim statement not a question, but she confirmed it anyway.

"No, he wasn't. But even if he had been, the wolf still would have killed him. It refused to have him as a mate no matter what. It was close, though." *Too close.* She tilted her head back, meeting his golden stare. "I don't want that to happen again. I can't," she paused, ready to put voice to the words but unwilling to go any further. "I can't lose my mate because she can't be controlled."

"What do you think she'll do?" he murmured.

Ronnie cupped his cheeks, enjoying the rough scruff that coated his jaw. "I think she'll lose control." She rubbed her chest. "There's so much anger here. So much fear. I worry she'll slip her leash and lose control. I worry she'll hurt you."

Braden snorted. "I'm offended that your wolf thinks she can beat me." It was his turn to sigh. "But I understand your hesitation and your worry." He placed a finger beneath her chin, forcing her to meet his stare. "And I want you to know that no one—*no one*—will ever make you do anything you don't want to do. Not while I'm breathing. You understand?"

She nibbled her lower lip and nodded, not sure if she could trust that. Could she lean on him? Let him be the one between her and the world?

The wolf said yes. The wolf wanted him. The wolf wanted his bite and wanted to howl and…

Ronnie snapped the trap closed on that thought.

"Veronica?"

"Yeah," she whispered. She understood and a tendril of hope unfurled. Part of her wanted to believe him, too.

"Good." He grunted and then quiet surrounded them. The silence comfortable and not oppressive. "I hate that I wasn't there for you."

"You didn't know me." She pointed out. "But I had my family, the pack."

"This is why you think it's a good idea for Claire to go to your mother."

She nodded. "Yes, she's... It's not the same, but my mom knows what it's like for a young girl to feel so..."

Broken.

Braden's hands were soft, his touch careful, as he stroked her. "Thank you for sharing this with me. For trusting me."

Another nod. She did trust him. So much. And that... surprised her. The wolf snorted and told her to catch up already. They'd trusted Braden for a while.

And maybe that was true. That didn't mean she was ready to push forward with a full mating though. Maybe not ever.

"You're my mate, Braden."

"I know."

"But I don't know if I can ever fully be your mate. I don't know that I can let my wolf go that far. I trust you. I don't trust her."

"And that's okay," he murmured. "Because I don't trust my traditions, my tiger. I don't trust what could become of my future if we tried to fully mate like other tigers in the prides."

Air wheezed from her lungs and her wolf bristled at her words. The truth though... the truth was that from his perspective, it was a valid fear. Ronnie knew her strengths, knew that she was a fierce wolf, but still a wolf. Smaller than a tiger. Not as strong. Some said not as quick.

Wolf still snarled though. "The wolf could take the tiger."

Braden rubbed his thumb across her lower lip before brushing his lips across hers. "Are you willing to lose me forever to test that belief? You won't risk losing me to your wolf. I won't risk losing you to my tiger traditions."

"Where does that leave us?"

"Exactly where we are. Wherever you want to be. I won't force this on you. I won't force a bite on you. They can roar and howl as loud as they want, but it's up to you—up to us."

Ronnie nodded, hearing and understanding his words. The future, their future, was in her hands. How far was she willing to go for him?

The ends of the Earth.

"I," she wet her lips, trying to put her thoughts to words. "I want to be yours. I want you to be mine. I want to share bites so others know you're mine, but the rest—"

"The part that could tear us apart."

"Yes, I think we should wait for that."

Forever.

CHAPTER THIRTEEN

If they didn't let him see Veronica soon, he'd kill someone. Or maybe more than one someone. They'd given him some time with his mate, but not enough. Not nearly enough. He'd held her close, dried her tears, and they'd agreed to mate. Then the women descended en masse. They swept in and shoved him out.

If he hadn't been flying high over getting her agreement, he would have fought harder. But, he was getting his way so he didn't give a damn.

That was hours ago.

He threw himself back into organizing the men, making calls and setting plans, ensuring everything Walter and Ares planned for the party and coming days were enough. He trusted the two alphas, but… Veronica was his mate.

The party was in full swing, pride members arriving early to try and get a peek at Veronica, but failing since *she wasn't at his side.*

He took a calming breath, releasing it slowly, and then took another sip of his beer, the cold brew sliding down easily and smoothly. There was a little something extra in there, a taste he couldn't quite put his finger on. Sweet yet savory, and he wondered…

"How you doing?" Ares came to his side and leaned against the porch railing.

"Fine." Why wouldn't he be? He had a mate, a protective pride, and a good life. "The question is, how are you doing?" He tipped his head toward the small cluster of women on the other side of the yard—a group of wolves surrounding one tigress. "And are you going to be okay?"

The alpha growled low, drawing the attention of one of the more timid tigers nearby, and the sound was silenced as quickly as it began. "I don't want her going anywhere. Not with anyone, not with them."

By "her," he meant Claire and by "them," he meant the wolves.

He could relate. The alpha—alphas since it was a surprise to Walter as well— had finally been told about the plan for Claire, about the tigress heading off to the Lakes while they waited to discover if the human transitioned.

"It'd be good for her," he murmured. "No one here has gotten through to her, you know. First time I heard her laugh was this morning with Veronica. I haven't seen her smile so much since Talia claimed her and has dragged her everywhere. Veronica's sisters have already brought her into their circle as family."

"I know," Ares grumbled. "But I can't protect her when she's with the wolves."

"They can handle it. She'll be in the alpha's house, not some random apartment. The beta and several sentinels live with him."

"She's so young. What if they—"

Braden snorted. "She's twenty-two. And a tigress. What happened with the human aside; she's a strong feline. Stronger since all that happened. I hate what was done to her, but she's a fierce bitch now. You need to see she can take care of herself physically. She needs emotional help." He took another sip, savoring the taste and still wondering why the hell it was so good. There really was something extra he couldn't quite pinpoint.

"We can help her."

"You're pouting like a woman."

"Fine, our cousins can help her."

"Uh-huh." Another sip that went down nice and smooth. He generally wasn't a big drinker, but this…

"Mom's uniquely qualified to help her, Ares. It's a good idea and she'll be safe." His mate's voice reached him, and some of his lingering tension fled.

Her footsteps were soft as she approached, and he lifted his arm, inviting her to snuggle against his side. She eased into his embrace without another word, and he tugged her even closer before dropping a kiss on the top of her head.

"Missed you," he murmured low and breathed in her scent. It went straight to his cock. A mating party organized by her parents seemed like a great idea, and he was behind the event… in a week. Maybe two. It would give him time to sate his need for her.

Unfortunately, thwarting Cadman involved their mating and having it recognized by others.

Hello, mating party.

Veronica chuckled. "You snuck in and saw me this morning."

Yeah, he had. It'd been painful but he sensed their bond growing stronger after their talk.

"And then your mother kicked me out," he grumped.

Ares coughed. "Not to interrupt—"

"But you're doing it anyway." Braden managed to keep his growl in check. Barely. His body was on fire for his mate, and talking to people just delayed his claiming even more.

"How is she uniquely qualified? What makes you guys think she has any idea what Claire is going through? How can she do something none of us can?"

Veronica nuzzled his chest, hiding her face, but she did answer. "Because someone close to her experienced something similar and my mother managed to keep the girl sane."

His mate's pain filled the air, earning more than one confused look, and he glared at his alpha.

"I see." Ares's expression told Braden he understood. Or at least could put a few pieces together.

He rubbed her back, tracing her spine in a gentle caress. The three of them remained silent—Braden sipping his beer, Ares enjoying soda, and Veronica clinging to him.

Wait, soda? The alpha enjoyed a good beer as much as Braden did. He flicked his gaze to the male's cup and then raised an eyebrow, causing Ares to roll his eyes.

"Zoe wants to have cubs soon-ish. Which means she refuses to drink alcohol, and if she can't drink alcohol…"

Braden snorted and shook his head. "Then you can't drink alcohol. Can't believe you agreed."

A small elbow collided with his side. "Hey, you're going to deal with the same thing eventually so enjoy that beer while you can."

He froze, heartbeat stuttering as he imagined Veronica swollen with his cub. Or pup? No matter what she had, she'd be beautiful, and their child would be just as precious. "Really?"

Braden took another sip. If it was going to be outlawed, he wanted to finish his drink first. Maybe more than one.

It was her turn to stiffen in his embrace. The scent of her nervousness slipped free of her pores. "Uh... I dunno. What answer are you looking for?"

He emptied his cup and set it on the railing, freeing up his hand so he could get both of them on her. He cupped her cheeks, encouraging her to meet his gaze. "I want to have a family with you. Today, tomorrow, a year from now. I want that."

"But our mating..."

"It'll be what it'll be. You have your reasons." At his words, her lips twisted into a grimace. "And I respect and understand them. I have my own, remember?" He still didn't trust his tiger even though it assured him she'd be a match for them and it would accept her. The animal was convinced she'd prove herself to be a good mate. "But our mating will be just that—ours. No matter what it is or what it becomes, I want to have a family with you when you're ready."

Her eyes glistened, moisture filling them for a moment before she blinked it away. "How'd I get so lucky?"

He grinned. "You haven't gotten lucky yet." He waggled his eyebrows. "Wanna?"

His joke had the desired effect, his mate snorting and then laughing aloud. "Dork."

"Hard as hell dork." He flexed his hips, making sure he rubbed himself against her softness.

Fuck, but he was hot for her. His mind wouldn't let go of thoughts of her spread beneath him, body welcoming his possession as he thrust in and out of her wet pussy. His dick twitched with the thought, and he swallowed the groan threatening to burst free. He burned for her, and his tiger roared, demanding he snatch her to him and carry her to their den. He could lock her in the room. Or rather, lock others out. Then he could strip her bare, lick, taste, and bite her until they were as tied as they could be.

She'd be his then. As bound as they could be without pushing his mate further than she wanted to go.

Veronica licked her lips, gaze dropping to his mouth, and he smiled. Soon the flavors of her nervousness vanished only to be replaced the musky scent of her arousal. Her nipples hardened and pressed against his chest, the fabric between them doing little to blunt the sensations. His mate was aroused, her body preparing for him, and he wanted nothing more than to strip her bare and fill her pussy. First he'd lap at her cream and savor each delicate morsel. She'd be so sweet on his tongue, a flavor he could quickly become addicted to.

Braden lowered his head, anxious to capture her lips since he couldn't exactly rip her clothes off and mount her with everyone nearby. Well, really, it was because her family was around. When it came to the pride, his tiger was more than happy to take Veronica in front of the crowd. The animal wanted every shifter to know she was *his*.

He didn't think her father wanted to see.

"Really? Can you, I don't know, keep your naughty thoughts to yourselves? We're in *public*." Zoe's words cut through his growing arousal.

He wanted to growl at the tigress but managed to suppress the sound. Veronica had no such compunction and snarled at her best friend.

"Like you two haven't been humping each other's legs."

"Touchy, touchy." Zoe held out two cups, one nearly overflowing with beer while the other was filled with some sort of dark liquid on ice. "Here, Daddy Walter wants to start the toasts soon. He's got a video camera guy hanging around too because he needs some good tape to send to the press in the morning. You know, us being human."

Veronica wrinkled her nose. "Black Wolf on ice?" He raised his eyebrows in question. "Sambuca, Green Chartreuse, and a little Tabasco. Wolves are sorta a fan of anise the way catnip gets feline motors running."

Catnip? Braden took a sip of his beer and turned his questioning expression on Zoe. That savory sweet he'd tasted in his last drink was present in this one as well. His tiger was tempted to get angry at being drugged, but the catnip was already doing its job. The cat told him they'd bitch about the catnip tomorrow. They felt too good right now.

The tigress shrugged and didn't apologize. "You two need to be friendly and act like newlyweds but you're both a little growly. Being the helpful, wonderful, amazingful alpha fem I am, I came bearing gifts."

"So you drugged us?" Veronica growled.

Zoe grinned. "You being pleasant is a sure thing now. Besides," she smirked. "You'll really enjoy yourselves now instead of just pretending."

"Zoe?" Walter's raised voice reached across the yard and the tigress nodded.

"C'mon. He hates waiting. Talia promised you just have to play nice through a few speeches, and then you can run off and do newlywed things."

Ares followed Zoe across the yard, leaving them a little space, and sank into his mate. Her scent, the musky sweetness, enveloped him. He breathed it in, loving and cursing the flavors at the same time. She made his dick rock hard, but she… made his dick hard. It was real damn difficult to move when his cock was being strangled by his pants.

"*Veronica!*" The alpha wolf's bellow reached them and they both winced. Apparently the wolf was done being ignored.

"Grab your drink. A few toasts and then we can find some privacy," Veronica murmured.

Braden glanced at the house, knowing all of the guest rooms were filled and then raised his eyebrows. "And that will happen how?"

"Privacy that may involve the forest," his mate chuckled. "Now, come on. The quicker we're done, the quicker we'll both get what we want." They took two steps and then she stopped, reaching out to squeeze his hand and grab his attention. "I… I've never felt this good. Not since…" she shook her head. "Not ever, actually. Like I can breathe. Thank you for that. For being you. For helping me be me."

"*Ver-on-i-ca!*"

The national wolf alpha was done waiting.

CHAPTER FOURTEEN

Ronnie didn't realize how much she giggled when she was drunk. Or that she found everything in the world hilarious. That initial Black Wolf had led to another. And then another. And then she sorta lost count because, like she told Braden, they really were like werewolf catnip.

And Braden... had ingested a lot of catnip. He said it was sweet and smoky and a wonderful complement to his beer.

Hours later, toasts complete, smiles flashed for cameras and video recorders, and howls and roars released in celebration, and Ronnie was ready for bed. So her mate could fuck her and... claim her? The wolf agreed, anxious for his fangs in her flesh, but could she trust the animal? It'd betrayed her once before. Would it again? What would it do to Braden?

Nothing, it assured her. The animal would never hurt their mate.

Ronnie shook her head. She wasn't ready to risk his life. She'd keep a lid on the wolf and wouldn't let it wrench control from her human body. Maybe someday, but not today—tonight.

Her mate tugged her close, his heavy arm draped across her shoulders, and she snuggled into his side, nuzzling his firm chest. He was so strong, so fierce. And even if her father refused to admit it, she knew he liked her mate. At least a little bit. He hadn't challenged Braden, so that was a plus. If her daddy really wanted him gone, he would have found a reason to kick Braden's ass. Since Braden's ass was hard under her hand and decidedly unkicked, she figured they were ahead of the game.

The last lingering tigers intent on wishing them well slowly made their way around the house and toward their cars. Which left her and Braden mostly alone in the backyard. Zoe and Ares cuddled beneath a nearby tree while some of the other couples who'd attended also found private places.

"How you feeling?" Braden nuzzled the top of her head and inhaled. "You drank a lot."

"Hmm…" Yes, she had, and it was delicious. "Good. Buzzed, but not really drunk. Just happy."

He hummed and then spoke once more. "So what comes next, if you're not really drunk and just happy?"

Ronnie's wolf was intrigued by the question and pushed to its feet inside her mind, padding forward and nosing her. "What do you want to happen?"

He chuckled. "No fair. Don't try and catch me in one of those women questions. Tell me what you want. Because I want you naked beneath me. I want you screaming my name. I want my teeth in your shoulder." He bent and nipped her shoulder. She tilted her head to the side and gave him more room. "I want yours in mine."

"Yes." Yes to all of that.

And more, the wolf assured her.

Ronnie swallowed hard, a hint of faith blossoming in her heart. Could she trust the animal? All she could remember from the last time she'd tried to get close to a man was pain and blood. Screams suddenly cut off by death.

"But I'm not doing this inside the house where everyone can hear every sound."

She giggled. Her. She *giggled*. "Forest it is. They can stumble over us, but I imagine whoever else is out there tonight is looking for privacy too." Ronnie scraped her fang over his skin. This was what she wanted, what she'd always wanted. Understanding. Support. Acceptance. They both had issues, they both had reasons, and they both wanted to be together in any way they could. Mates, but not, and that was okay. "Know any good spots?"

"I know plenty." He pulled back and his intent gaze met hers. "Are you sure?"

"More than. I want your bite, Braden."

The wolf wanted more.

The wolf could go fuck itself. She *would not* risk Braden. Ever.

He pressed a quick kiss to her lips, and she was glad he didn't try to take it deeper. She couldn't guarantee she wouldn't pounce on him if he had. Her pussy was wet—soaking—for him, and she couldn't wait to get naked. "Not solidifying our bond doesn't make it any less than another couple. It doesn't lessen my commitment and lov—" He cleared his throat. "C'mon. You wanna shift, or do you want skin."

Oh hell no. She grabbed his hand when he went to move away. "Nope, finish what you were gonna say."

"I have no idea what you're talking about." He even blanked his expression. Too bad for him shifters could scent emotions.

"Try again."

He grimaced.

"Here, I'll help you." She slipped her hands around his neck and pushed to her tiptoes until less than an inch separated their mouths. "Not solidifying our bond doesn't lessen my commitment and love for you." Those words rang true inside her. Their love wasn't overnight, but slowly established over the weeks she'd spent with him. It was strengthened by the recent adversity and hardened by their talk earlier in the day.

Braden was her mate, her other half. Her forever.

Ronnie nipped his lower lip. "Your turn."

"Veronica…" He tried to lean in and kiss her, but she jerked back.

"Nope, let's hear it. All of it."

Braden pressed his forehead to hers. "I love you. I want to mate you. I want you to be mine, and no matter how we form our bond, it's still going to be as strong and fierce as any others." He squeezed her tightly. "You're mine, Veronica Barrington."

"Veronica…" she swallowed hard, heart thumping a rapid beat as nerves assaulted her. Why was this part so difficult to say? She'd said everything else, but… She mentally growled and huffed. She wasn't a pussy even if she was mating a tiger. "Veronica Scott."

"As soon as we find a little moonlight and a nice patch of forest, you're mine." He moved away from her and she let him go, not objecting when he dragged her toward the forest.

He loved her. Her, a woman who'd killed a man for what they were about to attempt. The wolf snarled and told her she was an idiot. The animal wanted the tiger just as much as Ronnie ached for the human.

So maybe... maybe if a howl made its way up her throat, she'd release it.

Maybe.

The wolf said certainly. There was no maybe about it.

Ronnie decided she'd take a wait-and-see approach.

For now, she'd focus on getting naked and running through the woods with her tiger mate. He led her into the deep shadows of a large tree, not releasing her until they were out of sight.

"This a good spot for you?" His voice was deep and soothing, blunting some of the nervousness plaguing her.

She surveyed the area, peeking around the trunk and realizing she couldn't see any remaining partygoers. "Perfect." She smiled and turned back to her mate. Her very naked, very aroused, mate. She widened her eyes and her mouth dropped open with shock. "Oh shit."

He grinned. "Oh shit good, or oh shit bad?"

She licked her lips, gaze taking in every detail. The moon's light bathed him in a silvery glow that accentuated his muscled body. She'd traced each one of those carved lines while they were both clothed, from the firmness of his pecs to his rippled abs. His thick arms had cradled her gently, and those large hands caressed her with subtle passion while his strong legs supported her when she leaned against him. He was strength personified... and all hers.

"Oh shit, I bet you taste good." The visible V at his hips directed her to his cock, the closely cropped curls framing his thickness. He was long and firm, his dick seeming to point right at her as if to say, "Pick me, pick me!"

Which had her snorting and him frowning. "Laughing at a guy isn't the best confidence booster."

That had her grinning, and she shook her head. "You've got no reason to doubt your appeal." She rolled her eyes. "You know you're sexy as hell." She strolled forward, her hand immediately going to his chest. "You know I'm wet for you." She let her fingers trail down his body and over his abdomen. She traced each dip and curve, loving that her mate was so strong, so fierce. She teased the short hair around the base of his dick. Braden moaned, and when she encircled his shaft, the sound turned into a rumbling purr. She stroked him, enjoying the feel of his silken length against her palm. "You know I want you."

"Fuck, Veronica." His hips jerked and he thrust into the circle of her hand. "What you do to me."

What *he* did to *her* was more like it. He got her hot with a look, a smile, a whiff of his scent. She caressed him from base to tip, gathering the droplet of moisture that'd gathered there. She salivated and licked her lips, wondering how he'd taste. They'd shared kisses in the past but hadn't progressed to more intimate things. Now she could—she should, in fact.

"How close are the others?" she whispered. She hadn't paid attention to the rest of the lingering partygoers.

"Huh?" Passion-glazed eyes met his. "What?"

"Where is everyone else? Any other shifters nearby?" She pumped him once more, using his pre-cum as a lubricant.

"No," he shook his head and squeezed his eyes shut before opening them wide once more. "They're all gone. In the house or the woods."

"Good." She smirked, and her pussy clenched, anticipation thrumming through her veins. Her gums ached, her wolf asserting itself and assuring her the idea sounded like the best thing ever.

"Good?" When she brushed the tip of his dick with her thumb, her big, bad tiger whimpered.

Ronnie's lips tingled and her gums ached, her wolf pushing forward in anticipation. She slowly lowered to her knees, ignoring the dried leaves and pebbles pressing into her flesh. When her face drew even with his cock, nothing else mattered. "Yeah," she whispered, meeting his gaze as she flicked her tongue out and captured the next bead of pre-cum. "Good."

Chapter Fifteen

Good didn't cut it.

Shit, having Veronica's mouth on him was so beyond good he wasn't sure what he'd call it. Fucking fantastic wasn't strong enough.

Braden braced himself, feet shoulder-width apart and he wished he had a tree at his back to keep him upright.

Amber eyes met his, her irises dilated until most of the color was obliterated by the proof of her need. That wasn't the only clue to her arousal. The flavors of her desire filled the air, her body screaming for him. For his mouth, his hands, his cock. He knew he'd find her wet, her panties soaked as her cream seeped from her center.

She darted her delicate pink tongue out to lap at the tip of his dick, the wetness bathing the spongy head in a single lick.

"Veronica," he whispered hoarsely. She stole his breath and nearly all his control. She repeated the action, tip toying with his leaking slit. Her dark hair fell forward, and he immediately reached for the strands, brushing them back. "Want to see you. Need to watch you suck me. Fuck, so pretty."

He knew his tiger was out in full force, could sense the animal's presence, the burn of its fur as the hairs slid through his pores and the ache of his fingers from his beast's nails. If she were human, he'd worry about scaring her. Since his mate was a wolf, he let his inner feline out as much as he dared.

Veronica pulled the head of his dick into her mouth, lips parting just enough to accept him. She flicked the tip and then sucked his flesh, drawing his pleasure forward. His balls ached and pulsed, his body preparing to find the final bliss of release.

But not yet… not until…

She swallowed him, opening her jaws wider and sliding her mouth along his hard length. She took more and more of him, swallowing inch after inch and then retreating. His shaft glistened with her saliva, the night air cooling his skin. Then she accepted him once more, lips caressing his shaft.

Fuck, but she was beautiful, all amber eyes, tumbling hair, and heart-shaped face. She still wore clothing, but the neck of her shirt gaped, giving him a clear view of her plump breasts. He was desperate to get his hands on them, to suck and nibble her nipples just like she pleasured his dick. Her skin was pale in the moon's light and he knew it was as soft as it appeared. His mate was a deliciously wicked angel, and he couldn't wait to get her dirty.

She ran her nails up his thighs, the sharpened tips pricking his skin as she stroked him, and he shuddered at the hint of pain. His balls throbbed and his dick twitched in the depths of her mouth. That small bite drove his pleasure higher, the desire for her growing with each heartbeat. She was glorious in her passion, eyes filled with lust and need.

Veronica wrapped one small hand around his shaft, squeezing him gently, and then she stroked his dick as she sucked. Her hand worked in conjunction with her heavenly lips and tongue, driving him mad with the need for her.

Another hint of pain joined his pleasure, her nails scraping his thigh from knee to groin. She cupped his balls, holding them gently in her small palm. She squeezed softly and he shuddered, enjoyment from her touch jolting through him in an uncontrollable wave of sensation. Fuck it felt good. Good and bad at once because he was nowhere near ready to come. He wanted to do that balls deep inside her pussy, his fangs at her throat.

Soon. Not yet. But fucking soon.

She caressed his sack, fingers gentle on his sensitive skin, and he let the pleasure of the connection wash through him. His tiger purred, sounding out its approval, and the sound actually left him in a rolling rumble. The cat was pleased with their mate and couldn't wait to chase and pounce on her—make her theirs.

With the next glide of her lips along his shaft, she released him, hand continuing to stroke, yet her mouth was gone from his dick.

"Veronica," he whispered her name, unable to remain silent.

"Tell me what you want," she whispered just as softly.

"You. Always you."

Forever you.

Veronica opened once more, tongue darting out to catch his cum, and then she gently lapped the head, lulling him with the sensuous pleasure. She pulled back her lips, baring her fangs. Her wolf pushed forward and transformed her normal canines to her beast's—long and wicked. He remained motionless as she brought those deadly teeth close to his dick, not moving as she very carefully scraped the sharp edge over the spongy tip.

"Fuck," he hissed, shuddering with the unexpected pleasure. His tiger chuffed and roared its approval, loving their mate's possession of them.

She went back to sucking him, adding hints of pain with her fangs or nails, driving him mad with the need to come. Her hands never stopped caressing him, never stopped stroking his length or gently kneading his balls. He moaned and gasped with each new sensation, the pleasure gradually increasing with every breath. The impending ecstasy grew, blossoming with every heartbeat. It began at the base of his spine, the ball of bliss coalescing and then sliding along his nerves. His blood heated, warming with her touch, with the sounds of her moans and groans.

Through it all, she never stopped moving, never stopped touching him, fondling him, driving him crazy with her touch.

Braden cupped her cheek, rubbing her cheekbone gently with his thumb and then her lips where they stretched around his cock. "You know how beautiful you are. So mine. So perfect." She moaned, and the vibrations shot through him, racing along his skin and then spreading through his body. "Dammit, Veronica. Not gonna last." The little brat did it again, drawing the sound out, and his balls hardened and tightened against him. "You're gonna make me come. Wanna be in you the first time."

Grinning, she gradually released him, her hand continuing to stroke his cock as she rained gentle kisses along his shaft. "You can come in my mouth." She flicked him with her tongue, teasing just beneath the head. "That's in me." Next she sucked the spot and then scraped her fang over the sensitized tissue. "Isn't it?"

Fuck, she was killing him and she knew it. "Baby, want in your pussy the first time."

She hummed and drew him into her mouth once more in a sensuous slide of her lips over his soft skin. "Come in my mouth, Braden."

"Veronica." He would never admit he whined like a kid.

Those lips left him. "Do it." She kissed his slit. "Want to taste you before you fuck me." She scratched him with a single fang and he shuddered with the pleasure it caused. "Need it." Her next lick was a barely there teasing of her tongue. "Don't you want to give me what I need?"

"Fuck," he hissed, the two sides of him battling the urge to please her and pleasing himself. And really, pleasing himself ended with pleasing her since he couldn't think of anything but diving between her milky thighs. Whether it was to fuck her or taste her, he didn't know and didn't care.

"Give it to me," she whispered. "Now." That time her voice held the growl of her beast. His tiger bristled at the order, but then she swallowed him to the base, his cock hitting the back of her throat, and they both agreed she could do whatever the fuck she wanted.

Braden let her take control, let her torment and tease him as she desired. Her hands resumed their maddening taunts, stroking and petting him in a way that made his blood burn with need. Her mouth never stopped moving, lips gliding up and down his length, tongue teasing and driving him crazy with the random strokes.

And he reveled in it all. He let the passion fall onto him, his body accepting the impending release. The pleasure grew, increasing and morphing into a mass of ultimate joy that threatened to smother him in the sensations. He embraced the trembling waves of joy consuming him, letting them blanket him in a suffocating embrace.

His cock pulsed, balls throbbing, telling him his orgasm lingered at the edges of his mind and he'd come at any moment. "Veronica." She sucked hard and his knees went weak, pleasure snatching his strength. "Gonna…"

Her fingers moved, two easing behind his balls and pressing against that bit of skin between his sack and his ass and he nearly doubled over as he came. The pleasure slammed into him like a train, pulsing in his veins and burning his nerves with the bliss.

He shouted his enjoyment to the night, his roar booming through the darkness. He jerked and twitched as the bliss continued, overwhelming joy consuming him. Veronica didn't stop, didn't slow in her attentions as cum erupted from the head of his dick. His balls emptied into her mouth, and she swallowed each drop, her throat working and undulating as she took him within.

His yell subsided as the ecstasy ebbed, gradually lessening until his cock softened within her mouth. Fuck, but he needed her. Needed to touch her. Needed to taste her. Needed her naked and writhing beneath him for hours and hours.

But Braden couldn't do that when she was still fully clothed. He eased from her, gratified at her whimper when he retreated, and reached down. In one smooth move, he had her off her feet and in his arms. Without hesitation, he captured her lips, shoving his tongue into her mouth. She fought to pull away, but he didn't give a damn if he tasted himself. It was their shared passion, not only his. The scent of her arousal was an aphrodisiac, stealing his control and dictating his actions.

Their tongues twined as he explored her mouth, tasting every inch of her he could. He swallowed her delicate, sweet flavors and he felt himself responding to her once again. He wouldn't be denied, he was energized and anxious to take Veronica in any way he could.

He wrapped his arms around her, tiger's nails digging into the fabric, and he yanked, fighting to rid her of the shirt. Cloth kept her skin from his, and that was unacceptable. She moved, and he tightened his hold, unwilling to lose her, but then he realized she wasn't trying to get away—she was helping. She ripped at the covering as well, wolf's claws assisting him until they'd shredded her top. Her hard nipples branded him with proof of her desire, but that wasn't the part of her he craved the most. No, he wanted to drop to his knees and taste *her*. Fuck, she'd be salty and sweet and perfect on his tongue.

And it seriously needed to be soon. His cock was already slowly filling, hardening and thickening for her.

Braden wrenched his mouth from hers, panting against her lips. "Veronica. Need."

He didn't give a fuck that his vocabulary was limited. Not when his tiger rode him hard with a single demand.

Claim. Claim. Claim.

Then one single word boomed in his head.

Now.

CHAPTER SIXTEEN

Now.

Ronnie needed Braden *now*.

But on her terms.

Which meant when he leaned forward once more, his grip slowly tightening, she bolted. She ducked out of his hold and ran deeper into the forest. Her shirt and bra were tatters, the remnants easily tossed off. Her shoes were equally easy to kick away, the flip-flops giving her no trouble. The shorts were a different story and she was pissed she hadn't worn a dress to the party instead of something with a button and zipper.

Thankfully, she had claws.

One wrench turned into two, along with a long scrape of nails through the fabric and they too fluttered to the ground. Her panties soon befell the same fate, which left her racing through the tiger forest naked.

The sounds of snapping twigs, rustling bushes, and deep growls came in her wake. Her mate snarled and growled, obviously not liking being left in the dust. She heard him getting closer, and she increased her speed, racing for the one area Zoe said was beautiful and private without being too far from the house. It was the alpha pair's favorite place and her friend had promised to keep Ares away from the spot for a night.

Bushes scratched at her skin and twigs dug into her soles, but she pushed on. The wolf was enjoying the chase, of being her mate's prey as they dashed past trees and shrubs. She headed south, turning at the big boulder Zoe had talked about.

A curse came from behind her, her mate, obviously having to slip and slide before changing direction. A giggle escaped her lips before she could suppress it, and Braden snarled in response.

"Veronica," he rasped, the tiger filling his voice.

Another laugh burst past her lips, and she leaped into the small clearing, stumbling to a stop and then spinning to face her oncoming mate. He rushed into the flat area but didn't halt as she did. No, in fact, he pounced on her. He snatched her close, rolling them in the air so he took the brunt of their fall.

She laid atop him, skin to skin, and she gloried in the feel of his warm body snug with hers. They'd laid together at night, snuggling on the couch when she was too afraid to take things further. There would be no stopping tonight. Well, mostly.

The wolf purred, telling her they would do everything before morning. It was ready to take what belonged to them. Period.

Ronnie swallowed hard, unease slithering into her veins, and Braden stiffened. The lust filling his gaze slowly cleared, and his confused eyes met hers. "Veronica? What's wrong?"

She shook her head. "Sorry. Nothing. Just worried about…"

She swallowed hard. *About my wolf deciding you'd make a good snack.*

"Lovemaking and bites, remember? Nothing more." He placed a hand on her upper back and encouraged her to lower again. He nipped her shoulder, sending a sting through her but not drawing blood. "Lovemaking and bites."

A tendril of pleasure snaked down her spine, and a shudder followed in its wake. "Lovemaking and bites," she whispered her agreement.

Braden growled low, a sound that went straight to her pussy, and slowly flipped them until she rested on the damp grass. The blanket of green was soft and thick.

He rose above her and nudged her knees apart, kneeling between her spread thighs. "Fuck, do you know how beautiful you are?" He reached for her, his rough fingers sliding over her skin. The touch tickled before transforming into an arousing caress.

He started at her breasts, large hands cupping the mounds and he rubbed his thumbs around her nipples. He captured one and then the other between forefinger and thumb, pinching the hardened nub gently. It sent a new fire through her blood, causing her to burn with pleasure from within.

He slid his palms along her ribs to her waist to the flare of her hips. "Gorgeous." He caressed her legs to her knees before shifting to her inner thighs. "So soft and sweet, aren't you?"

His touch drew nearer to her center, his fingers tracing small circles on her heated flesh, and she whimpered when he stopped short of touching her pussy.

"Braden," she whined.

"Right here," he purred, and she wondered what it'd be like to have him purr against her pussy. "Not going anywhere."

"You're not doing anything either," she whined. Again. And she didn't give a damn if she sounded like a little kid. She wanted him to touch her pussy dammit.

"I'm definitely doing something." Golden eyes focused on her. "I'm learning my mate's body." He ran a single thumb along her slit, and her breath caught. "Like the fact a soft touch makes you gasp."

"Braden," she gasped as he delved between her labia and stroked her soaked sex.

"Right here. Touching you. Learning you."

"You could learn inside me," she cajoled. She wanted him thrusting in and out of her pussy. Now.

He brought his thumb up to her clit and circled the small bundle of nerves. "You don't want my mouth here? Touching you? Tasting you? Making you scream my name?"

As tempting as it sounded, she didn't want that. Yet. "In me. Please. You can do all that in round two."

He chuckled and leaned back, withdrawing his hand. He grasped the base of his dick and stroked himself, revealing he was already hard for her once again. "Is this what you want?"

Ronnie nodded. "Yes." She raised her gaze to him. "Now."

"Pushy wolf."

"Anxious wolf." She grinned at him and pushed to her elbows. "Slow tiger. Getting old already? Not up to the challenge of—"

Braden pounced, pushing her back to the ground as he covered her. "You want me? This? Us?"

"More than anything."

He tilted his hips and the blunt head of his dick slid through her cream, slickening his length. It took one pass, then two, and on the third he placed the blunted tip against her opening. "Say it."

"What?"

"You know." He stared at her, willing her to answer, and she knew what he wanted.

So she gave him what he desired. She gave him what they both desired. "Mate me. Claim me."

In once fierce thrust, he filled her, sliding in deep and causing her pussy to stretch around his intrusion. He consumed her with a single dive, claiming her body with his own. But it was only the first step.

There was more to come, and she couldn't wait.

Braden didn't stop until their hips met, his cock fully within her sheath, and their bodies completely joined. "Mine," he snarled.

"Yours," she arched her back and sought to take more of him.

"Shit, you're tight. Hot. Wet."

"For you," she moaned and rocked her hips. "Only for you."

"Forever for me." His growl was low and long, stretching into the night.

"Yes." She slid her hands along his arms, up his biceps, and across his shoulders before twining them around his neck. "Now make it real."

He took her words to heart, carefully retreating and slowly pushing forward once more with a gentle thrust and continued, careful movements that aroused her and drove her crazy at the same time. He slipped in and out again, his veined shaft stroking her inner walls. He touched nerve endings she hadn't realized existed, caressing her in a way that stole her breath.

Her wolf chuffed and whined with the growing pleasure, dancing in her mind and prancing in anticipation of their claiming. Their claiming?

Ronnie didn't have time to consider the words. Not when he increased his pace and added force behind each thrust. Her breasts jiggled with his strength, her body taking whatever he gave. She was his to use, his to pleasure, his to claim.

Her fingers burned, her wolf coming out further, and her gums ached as her fangs descended. Her mouth watered with the need to taste his blood, just as she'd tasted his cock, his cum. He'd been salty and sweet and she wondered if the rest of him was the same.

She'd find out. Soon.

His pace gradually increased, sending her spirals of pleasure soaring higher with each collision of their hips. He rubbed against her clit, and her pussy tightened and spasmed in response. She milked his length, squeezing and releasing as the ecstasy of his penetration continued to grow.

Her moans and groans warred with his, their bodies meeting in a rhythmic slap of skin on skin. The bliss of his lovemaking continued to grow, to stretch and fill every inch of her nude body until she thought she'd burst from the strength. But she didn't. No, somehow she was able to take more of the impending joy, able to accept more of the pleasure he caused until she wasn't sure if she would be able to breath any longer.

"Veronica. Mine." He bared his fangs and she noted the peppering of orange and black fur on his cheeks. Her wolf responded in kind, pushing gray strands through her skin. The animal wanted to match Braden step for step in his transformation, refusing to be left behind by their tiger mate.

"Yours." She groaned and planted her feet on the ground, using the new position to bring her hips to meet his. "You're mine."

"Fuck yes, yours," he hissed at her then, and she responded with her own rumbling growl from the wolf.

The animals crept closer and closer to the edge of their humans' control, stretching the leash that kept the animals contained within their skin. The wolf wanted to peer at their chosen mate, look him over and ensure he was worthy of… her howl?

But…

Braden growled and hissed again, a droplet of his sweat falling to paint her chest. He panted and huffed, body moving against hers as they both fought for release. They'd come, they'd claim, and then they'd revel in each other's bodies for the rest of the night. Ronnie met each of his movements, the wolf helping her along as they rocked and writhed.

The pleasure in her veins continued to blossom and grow. It stretched and pushed, sneaking into every inch of her body. Her nerves thrummed with her impending release, the bliss caused by Braden preparing to overflow and crash over her. Her clit twitched, her pussy clenching around him again and again.

"Braden. Want to…"

She wanted to come. Wanted to bite him and scream his name and more…

"Do it. Come on my cock, baby. Lemme bite you." Another snarl, another hiss, another ripple of fur sliding free of his pores.

Her wolf responded in kind, pushing out even more until she worried her jaw would snap and reform to her beast's.

"Do it."

She shouldn't have worried. Not when she had her mate deeply within her and issuing orders. She immediately responded to his words. Her body trembled, her back arched, and she screamed into the skies. His name left her lips, echoing into the night while pure ecstasy overcame her in a blinding wave of pleasure.

She jerked and twitched, body no longer her own as the bliss consumed her from inside out.

Consume.

Her mouth watered. She was supposed to...

Ronnie's wolf snatched control, and she tightened her hold on Braden's shoulders a split second before she pulled herself up and latched onto the juncture of his neck and shoulder with her fangs. She bit, his blood welling to the surface within a moment, and then she drank deeply. She sucked on the wound, feeling the initial mating bond settle into place. It allowed her to sense his feelings, know what went on inside his heart without hearing his thoughts. Joy suffused him along with a craving she recognized well. He wanted to bite her. Claim her. But he wanted her to release him first so he had a better angle.

His hips still continued to pump as he fought for his own release. Ronnie slipped her fangs free of his skin and lapped up blood. The wolf was pleased with itself, overjoyed at the injury they'd caused. It would scar and no one could doubt they were well and truly mated now. He belonged to her. He was...

On his next thrust, Braden sank his fangs into her flesh, sending a wave of pain down her spine. But on the heels came… bliss. Pure, unadulterated, unfamiliar, and overwhelming pleasure.

Ecstasy so great, so mind-blowing, that Ronnie opened her mouth, prepared to shout her joy to the skies.

But a shout wasn't what escaped. No, her wolf leaped to the fore at that moment, at the very second she released the deep breath and her yell transformed into a howl. It echoed through the air, consuming every hint of oxygen in the clearing, and she sensed their bond tightening further. Her wolf reached for the cat's soul, learning the intricacies of the mate. It knew the tie wasn't complete, but it reveled in what they'd created with Braden. The sound went on and on, her oxygen never seeming to run out as she released her pleasure.

She wasn't sure how long it took—moments or minutes—but Braden soon followed her. He released her shoulder and roared to the heavens, announcing his final release. Their voices joined, a wolf's howl and tiger's roar, volume increasing and encircling them with the purity of their claiming.

Their incomplete claiming. Her wolf accepted Braden wholly now, but as for his tiger… The animal would need to see that her beast was a match for his.

Actually, the animal would do nothing because Braden was suddenly ripped from her, his body thrown across the clearing. He rolled once over the grass before popping to his feet in a low crouch.

At that point, she noticed several things at once: a knife stuck out of her new mate's shoulder, and the human who put it there stood less than five feet away.

CHAPTER SEVENTEEN

Fire burned Braden's shoulder, the ache spreading with every beat of his heart. It raced through his veins like a river of lava, and he hissed long and low, the sound a combination of his pain and a threat to the male who'd attacked him. The weight of the blade pulled at his flesh, and he reached behind him, tugging the knife free. He tossed it aside, ignoring the sudden flow of blood down his back. The tiger didn't give a damn about pain—his own pain. It was too concerned with *causing* pain in another. Quickly.

This stranger had interrupted his mating, destroying what would have been a tender moment between new mates. Now the memory would forever be tainted with violence.

What was a little more?

He crouched low, pushing past the agony consuming his nerves, stared at his attacker, and faltered.

Braden recognized the enraged male, had studied his face as he lay near death in a bed in the pride house before being ambulanced to a nearby hospital. *He was in ICU.* Except he wasn't. He was glaring at Braden after stabbing him and interrupting his mating to Veronica.

What... How... Braden had *seen* him bleeding, barely breathing, in the den. *Seen. Him.*

His tiger purred, ignoring Braden's confusion. This was *perfect.* He'd been angry he hadn't been allowed to kill the male for threatening and injuring Veronica. Now he had his chance at retribution.

A shifter could defend itself from attack.

He snarled at the male, remaining low as he sifted through his options. Or rather, decided how best he wanted to kill the attacker.

Slowly, the cat demanded.

Yeah, yeah, he knew. The animal wanted to play with its food first.

"C'mon, beast. Let's go. You killed my brothers, and now I'm gonna get you." The man's hands shook, trembling as they faced off. Fear rolled off him in waves, reaching out to the cat, and the animal reacted to the scent. His tiger wanted to chase the human and scare him a little more. His attacker reached behind him and withdrew another blade, this one larger than the other. It glinted in the moonlight, the sharpened edge reflecting the glow. "Let's dance, kitty." .

The man sounded so different than he had on the side of the road. The stutter was gone, though the terror remained. The tiger reminded him that even the brave could feel fear.

Yeah, but there was something else…

"Do you only fight if your women are at risk? That it? Do I need to stab her so you stop being a pussy?" The human cackled and lunged for Veronica.

His mate scrambled backward, stark terror written across her features as she crawled out of reach. But that didn't stop the attacker. He jumped for her once more, barely missing her leg, and she bolted around a tree.

Braden leaped, putting his larger body between the human and his mate. One shove sent his attacker flying backward and sliding on his ass on the damp grass. He didn't stay down for long, though. No, he jumped up and bounced on the balls of his feet, wide eyes focused entirely on him.

But there was something odd in the stranger's gaze. His pupils were dilated, the black taking up the color of his irises. Drugged?

And his features… were they sharper? More angular? Was that fur…

"That's what I want." The human grinned. "Let's do this. I'm gonna kill you, and then I'll get her."

His tiger shoved forward then, refusing to be denied the joy of destroying the stranger.

Get Veronica? No.

He flexed his hands, claws emerging in a rapid flow of broken bones and deadly claws. His nails turned black, the cat taking full possession. "Never."

Braden stalked his opponent, his steps slow and measured as he approached the male and they began their violent dance of death. He still pulsed with pain, his knife wound seeping blood that slid down his body to soak the grass. He kept his hands loose, the tiger waiting for its chance to break free and snap the neck of their prey. It wondered what human would taste like, and he hoped he could restrain the beast so they wouldn't find out. He wasn't into cannibalism.

At all.

Cat told him he couldn't claim to hate something if he hadn't ever tried it.

Then their conversation came to a quick end, the honed blade heading toward Braden. He countered the attack, blocking the strike and returning the attempt on his life. He swiped the human's stomach, claws dug into skin and flesh. The scent of fresh blood filled the air and his mouth watered.

Fucking cat.

The wound had the human scrambling away, staggering backward, but his expression told Braden he wasn't done. He wasn't going to give up.

"Motherfucker," his attacker hissed.

The tiger decided the hiss meant his opponent wasn't human and actually had a little feline in him, so if he ate a tiny bit of the male while he was human-shaped… would that still be cannibalism?

Fucking cat.

Before the human could recover, Braden went on the offensive. He lunged and swung, claw digging into the male's thigh and only stopping when his nails hit bone. The wail was near deafening, piercing his eardrums. But he wasn't going to stop. Not yet. He still clung to the knife, still swept his arm in a wide arc as if to slice him.

Fuck that.

Braden attacked again, grasping his knife hand and dug his claws into the male's bicep. The paleness of the human's upper arm was easily revealed and more blood flowed. When he attempted to punch Braden with his free hand, he elbowed the male in the face. A quick jab had him rearing back. Now his opponent bled from his nose as well.

The bloody knife went tumbling to the grass and Braden shoved the human away, unwilling to get any more of the coppery fluid on his skin. Everywhere it touched burned him, the pain slightly less than the agony still encircling his shoulder and slowly wrapping around to encompass his chest.

"No, you were supposed to die," the human wheezed. "He said…" His attacker tripped again, falling to his ass. "He said…"

Braden didn't have an ounce of pity for the male as he bled onto the green grass beneath him. In fact, the cat craved more. It wanted to paint the clearing in the human's blood, soak the dirt with the life-giving fluid until the man was dry.

"He who?" he rumbled.

"He…"

"Who?" he snarled and bared his fangs, the teeth now over an inch long and sharp enough to pierce skin and rip flesh. "Who predicted my death?"

"P-p-poison…" the human whimpered, his face growing paler by the second. "He gave me a shot and I'm stronger. Faster. He…" He gave up and finally lost consciousness.

The snap of bushes and crunch of leaves announced a newcomer—newcomers—and Braden searched the clearing for Veronica. He found her tucked behind a tree, her pale face and fear-filled eyes focused on him. He raced to her side, attacker forgotten, and yanked her to her feet. He wasn't in any shape to come up against another attacker. His body was on fire. Whatever poison the human had used now consumed him from inside out. "C'mon. We have to find—"

"What the fuck?" Ares's voice boomed through the air, and Braden whipped his attention to the tiger alpha.

A sense of relief filled Braden. His alpha was near. Gannon, Murphy, and Daniel came into view. They'd stand with

Veronica. They'd keep her safe from whatever new threat emerged. Because Braden? He was losing the battle to stay upright. Every beat of his heart encouraged him to fall to his knees and succumb to the poison filling his system.

"Ares?" The alpha strode toward Braden. "Keep her safe."

Small fingers, tiny claws digging into his skin, clutched him. "Braden?"

He focused on his mate and black spots marred his vision. "Let him keep you safe."

"Braden?" She squeezed him harder, and he realized he was slowly giving her his weight.

He'd crush her if he wasn't careful. That thought had him tearing from her hold and staggering away. "Ares, don't let anything happen to her."

His alpha caught him just as his knees gave out, and the darkness eased even closer. It knocked on the door to his tiger's den in his mind, the poison attempting to consume his inner beast as well. If it got to both sides of him, if it managed to destroy the other part of him... He didn't know what would happen to him then. "Ares..."

"She'll be safe. We'll keep her safe. Let's take care of you first."

Veronica dropped to her knees beside him. "Braden?"

He was losing the battle against the poison. He knew it, and there was nothing he could do. He blindly reached for her, sighing in relief when she tightly held his hand. "I would have mated you." He coughed and fought for air. "Tiger wanted you to pull his tail."

A droplet of water, cool and sweet, fell onto his skin. "I still will. I'm gonna kick his ass and pin him. No way he's getting away from my wolf."

He grinned. At least he thought he did. "It would have been fun."

"It *will* be fun."

"Get Mark over here. Now!" Braden was sure Ares bellowed, but it sounded like a whisper.

Her optimism was nice. Misplaced, but nice. He could feel his heartbeat slowing, the flow of his blood easing. Whatever the plan had been, it worked. Veronica had claimed him as her mate but now she'd be single again once he died. He hated leaving her alone, without protection, without his love. He wondered what their cubs would have looked like. Would they have had her hair and his eyes? Would they have stripes? He imagined a blue-eyed tigress with her fire and his strength. Sassy and brassy.

That thought had his grin widening. "We would've had pretty cubs, huh?"

She squeezed him harder. "We still will, but they'll be pups." Another tear. "Where the fuck is the doctor?"

"Did I kill him? Don't let Ares do it." He needed to stay alive. They had to question the human.

"No, I won't. I'll do it myself." She brushed the hair off his face. Her hands were so soft.

"No. Question… him." Saying the words was so hard. Why were they so hard?

"Braden?"

He fought to breathe and realized his problem. He wasn't breathing. He couldn't move his arms anymore. He couldn't move *anything*.

"Braden?"

Was his heart beating?

"Braden?"

No. No, it wasn't.

Chapter Eighteen

Braden was alive.

But so was the human.

Which meant Veronica was torn between staying at her mate's side and slitting the throat of the man who recovered in the other room. The same human who was supposed to be in critical care at the local hospital. Obviously he'd escaped, and his injuries weren't what'd been reported. That was something no one could understand. At least, not yet.

When they were attacked on the road, the human had run into the forest. When questioned, Murphy recounted every strike and cut he'd put on the male before carrying him to the SUV. Hell, even the reports from non-shifter doctors outlined a plethora of injuries. He'd been on the verge of death. And then he was suddenly wielding a poison-coated knife in the middle of tiger land.

And he still had the same goal—taking her.

Braden had protected her, defended her and fought for her. And he nearly lost his life for it.

The need for retribution burned hot inside her, the wolf craving the blood of the male in the other room. But she couldn't bring herself to leave her mate's bedside. He still lived, still breathed, but he was weak. Mark—the pride doctor— assured her he'd make a full recovery. The poison had been strong, but known to them. It made the term "death by chocolate" a reality. Not actual chocolate but one of the chemicals found in it that affected a feline's body to the point of death.

Her mate had received a highly concentrated dose from the human's blade, and it had killed him. At least for a short time. Now his heart beat, and his lungs worked to keep air flowing in and out.

She hadn't seen his eyes yet, though. She wouldn't be able to relax until she met his gaze, until he said her name. Hell, until he said anything.

"Ronnie?" The deep voice drew her attention from Braden, and she fought back the growl threatening to burst past her lips. The wolf was on edge, and it hated anyone who intruded on her time with her mate.

She turned and focused on Mark. Mark, the pride healer. Mark, the male who'd kept her mate alive. Mark… who'd get his ass kicked if he didn't leave her alone. "Yeah?"

"How's he doing?"

He hasn't woken up. How do you think he's doing?

At least, that's what she wanted to say, but she refrained. Antagonizing the doc wasn't going to make Braden heal any quicker. "No change."

Mark eased into the room, unwinding his stethoscope from his neck and putting the ear tips in place. He laid the diaphragm on her mate's chest, silently listening for a moment before moving the instrument around. When he was done, he unhooked the device from his ears and gave her his attention. "His heart's strong and lungs are clear." The healer glanced down Braden's body and she followed his gaze. She'd wiped away the excess blood, revealing pale skin. Pale, *unmarred* skin. "He's healing well."

"When will he wake up? Why won't he?" *Will he?* Was a better question.

"When he wants to. We counteracted the poison and flushed it out of his system. He just needs to recover now."

She gritted her teeth, swallowing the snarl. She'd done a lot of that since they'd brought Braden into the den. She'd bared her fangs, growled, and grumbled at anyone who got too close to him or who didn't give her the answers she sought. Such as when the fuck her mate would wake up.

"Is there anything I can do to move things along?"

Mark frowned. "You might be able to—"

"Ronnie?" More interruptions, from another male, but at least this one was Ares. When she gave the alpha her attention, she saw her father also stood at Ares's side.

She cleared her throat. "Yeah?"

"His attacker is awake."

Her gums throbbed as her wolf leaped to the front of her mind. The attacker was awake, which meant he could face justice. She could rip out his throat for harming Braden. She could bathe in his blood, and...

Her human mind wrenched control from the beast.

No. She wasn't doing that. They'd done it once before, and her soul couldn't handle another stain. "What did he say?"

"We haven't questioned him yet. Do you want to be there?"

Yes.

"No." She reached for Braden's still hand. "I don't want to leave his side. Will you tell me what you find out?" Her gaze eased from Ares to her father. "Daddy?"

"You know we will, baby girl," Walter's voice was gruff and filled with emotion.

She did know.

Her father eased past the tiger leader and slowly made his way to her. When he reached her side, he did the one thing no alpha ever did—he knelt for her, for family. "When we're done, it's your kill, sweetheart."

Her kill. She squeezed her eyes shut. It was her opportunity for vengeance. If a shifter couldn't avenge themselves, their mate was allowed to step in. Even though her wolf scratched and scraped in her mind, telling her to take the chance, she shoved it away. She stared at her hands, burgundy stains around her cuticles. "I've had too much blood today. Can you... Or Mom?"

Bears didn't have the corner on fiercely protective mothers. Talia Barrington would be all too happy to avenge her daughter and her daughter's mate.

"Of course. We didn't want to step on any toes." He leaned forward and pressed a soft kiss to her forehead. "You watch over Braden. We'll handle the rest. You help your mate get better. I can't threaten to gut him if he hurts you if he's not around. Threatening an unconscious man ain't no fun."

Ronnie chuckled and shook her head, the first ghost of a smile she'd had since entering the house. "You can't mess with him until he's on his feet."

He just grunted as if to say *watch me* and stood. A strong hand gently squeezed her shoulder before he stepped to her side.

The light patter of someone approaching reached their ears a brief moment before Darcy came into view.

The tigress flashed her a sad smile before looking at the tiger leader. "We have DoPE agents at the front door, Alpha."

Ares sighed, her father grumbled, but a growl even louder than the other two filtered through the room. When all four people stared at her with wide eyes, she realized it was her.

As soon as she recognized it, she swallowed the sound with a wince. "Sorry."

Her dad ran his hand through her hair, and she tilted her head back to meet his stare. "Always said my girl had grit. You're gonna be okay."

She nodded in agreement. "Yeah. As long as he wakes up, I will. If I find out DoPE had anything to do with our attack, though…"

No one could hide behind badges and acronyms.

"We'll figure it out." He released her and strode to the doorway. "Stay here. As soon as we know something, we'll tell you. For now, focus on your mate. Let us deal with the rest."

Ares and Darcy departed, Walter on their heels.

"Daddy?" He paused and looked back at her with eyes so like hers. "Thank you."

He rapped his knuckles in a silent goodbye and then disappeared from sight. With them gone, she gave Mark her full attention. "You said I might be able to do something? When I asked if there was a way to speed things along?"

Mark nodded, eyes raking over Braden before turning to her. "Yeah, I can't guarantee it'll do anything, but a mate connection goes deeper than even an alpha's tie to his pride or pack."

And they all knew he didn't respond to his alpha at the moment. Ares had tried to order her mate to wake, but Braden remained motionless.

"What do you want me to do?"

Mark rubbed the back of his neck, a blush tinting his cheeks. "Get in bed with him," he cleared his throat. "Naked."

Ronnie jerked back. "I'm not about to—" She wasn't going to try and have sex with her mate while he was out of it.

"No, no," he shook his head. "It's just, if you're successful, he'll want to, *you know*."

His cheeks blazed and she chuckled. "You're a healer, and you're blushing."

"I fix broken bones. I don't hold sex ed classes." He narrowed his eyes. "My idea is you give him some of your blood—from the vein through a needle, however. But sharing it is sexual with tigers." He raised his eyebrows as if to ask if it was the same with wolves, and she nodded. "So if you give him your blood and he wakes, he's going to want to do more than lie there. He'll want you." He ran a hand through his hair and then down his face. "I can't even guarantee it'll work. I'm just saying if it does, you should be ready. He'll be weak, but it won't stop a tiger. Especially not one as strong as the national second."

Ronnie focused on her mate, at his unmoving form beneath the thin sheets. She'd do anything to wake him—anything. Giving him a little blood and fucking him if he happened to open his eyes? Pfft. That was nothing. And if he wasn't on his deathbed, it'd be damn near enjoyable.

With a nod, she pushed to her feet and reached for the button on her shorts. "I'll give it a shot."

"Okay," he stood as well. "I'll clear out and tell the others they're barred from the room. As long as you don't need me, I'll—" A loud roar shook the den and Mark sighed. "I was going to be across the hall, but it sounds like Ares—"

Another roar, but this one was the tiniest bit different. "And my father," she added.

"Are going to tear into someone. If I'm not in my room, I'll be patching up whoever they're about to beat on." Mark left and headed toward the source of the snarls and growls, and the door closed behind him with a soft *click*.

"Well, baby, it looks like it's you and me for a while," she murmured to the unconscious Braden. It took no time for her to strip down, and then she eased under the covers. She snuggled up to his side, sighing with the feel of his skin on hers.

Once she was comfortable, her head on his pillow and their bodies aligned, she lifted her wrist to her mouth. Any injury she gave herself wouldn't normally last long, her wolf rushing forward to heal her.

The animal assured her it'd drag its ass when it came to healing this time. Braden was more important than dealing with some torn skin. It would help her with shifting her teeth, too. Her gums throbbed, flesh pulsating with a growing ache, and her fangs extended. They lengthened and sharpened, pricking her lower lip.

The beast had done enough. Now it was time for her human half to get with the program. She lifted her wrist, opened her mouth, and bit. Blood quickly welled to the surface, flowing past her lips, and she moved her injured arm to Braden's mouth. She pressed it firmly against him, squeezing her fist to encourage a greater flow.

"Come back to me…"

CHAPTER NINETEEN

Braden couldn't decide if he was in heaven or hell.

Hell because he was being teased by his mate's scent, but he couldn't move to wrap her in his arms and hold her close.

Heaven because her blood filled his mouth, coasting over his tongue and down his throat. His tiger purred, encouraging him to swallow and hunt for more. He tried and then tried again, but his throat refused to work, refused to take in more. So he *was* in hell then.

The tiger snarled, demanding he *do* something. Was he gonna lie there like a pussy? Get off his ass already. What the fuck?

But he was in hell... right?

The beast fought its bindings, ripping and tearing at its chains, digging into the earth and using his strength to pull away from the ropes that held it at bay. A roar shook his head, vibrating from within.

"Come back to me..."

Wait. He knew that voice.

"Please..."

It almost sounded like she was begging. She shouldn't ever have to plead with him. Unless he toyed with her and denied her pleasure.

"I need you…"

Of course she did. His tiger agreed, puffing out its chest.

"Come back to me…"

Huh, had he gone somewhere?

"Braden, wake up."

He snorted—mentally at least—he wasn't sleeping. He was *dead.* There was a difference.

"Dammit, Braden."

His mate was pissy in hell. But then she sobbed. Sobbed and collapsed against him, her tears raining onto his shoulder. The scent of her pain burned his nose. It called to his tiger, the animal unable to do anything but react to Veronica's call. It broke free of its bindings, barreling through his mind and demanding he respond to her—their mate.

He came to in a rush, a headlong leap into consciousness that had his back arching and his lungs expanding as he gasped for air. He fought for oxygen, his muscles tight as he arched and rose off the bed. He opened his eyes wide, taking in the room from his altered position, but it was that single voice and delicious flavor that brought him down. He slumped to the mattress, exhausted from the whip-fast rise from slumber. His heart raced, threatening to burst from his chest, and he struggled to get it under control. Blood pounded in his ears, silencing the world around him, but there was no shutting out one voice, one scent, one touch.

Small hands clung to him, tiny nails digging into his skin but not breaking the surface. She shuddered with each sob, and her tears soaked his shoulder.

"Mate," he rasped, mouth reluctant to form the single word.

She lifted her head, bloodshot eyes meeting his. "Oh, God, you're awake." She leaned over him, one hand going to his cheek. "You're awake."

"Thought I was dead." His voice was rough and scratchy.

Veronica sniffled. "You were, for a little while." She ran her fingers down his chest, digits skating over his skin, and a shudder racked his body. "But you're not anymore, and you're awake."

A trail of cool wetness lingered in the wake of her touch, and he frowned, a memory niggling his wandering mind. He reached for her hand, movement sluggish, but he managed to catch her. He brought it into his line of sight and frowned. "What did you do?"

"Mark said it might wake you," she whispered, and he couldn't suppress his whine.

The flesh was ragged, ripped with uneven edges as if she'd gnawed on herself to keep the wound open. "Baby…"

Braden couldn't leave her that way, hated that it might scar and burden her with the memory for the rest of their lives. He brought her wrist to his mouth and gently lapped at the wound. He gathered the flavors of her blood, but instead of focusing on the deliciousness, he concentrated on caring for her. A mate's saliva could heal some wounds, and he wanted to speed the healing of Veronica's as much as possible. "You shouldn't have, my mate."

"I needed to see your eyes, needed to know you were okay. Your body is healed, but you wouldn't…"

He hummed against her skin and licked her again. His body reacted to her closeness, the sweetness of her blood, and her glorious scent. His heartbeat increased, slowly coming back to life and returning to normal. His sluggish mind gradually sharpened with each lap of her flesh. "I'm here now."

He wasn't in hell. He was in heaven. His body healed and his mate in his arms.

He shifted on the bed, changing position until his free arm snaked beneath her so she could turn his shoulder into a pillow. Not just his mate, his *naked* mate.

Braden's body reacted. His cock twitched and slowly filled, a different kind of need for her blossoming within his blood. It heated for her, warming and rushing through his veins. She wiggled in place, and the musky flavors of her arousal slithered into the air. She responded to him as well, her pussy growing damp and preparing for him. They'd been interrupted by the male, their afterglow stomped on when the human…

Human.

"Where is he?" His arousal vanished and a growl took its place.

"The human?" She didn't even try to feign ignorance.

"Yes," the growl remained, the tiger demanding retribution. "Want him."

Wanted to kill him. Carve him into tiny pieces and feed him to the natural animals in the forest. Wanted to rain pain on the male until he begged for death. Unless he already had perished from the injuries in their fight.

"Is he still alive?"

Veronica sighed. "He is. Mark patched him up."

"Good." He released her hand and tensed, tightening his abs so he could sit up. "That means I can have fun killing him."

"Wait." She placed her palm on his chest and pushed him back down. Okay, maybe he wasn't as strong and recovered as he thought. "Ares and Daddy are interrogating him. Or they were supposed to. DoPE agents showed up a while ago. I'm not sure what's happened since then."

If they took his prey... "I'll kill them all."

Those delicate fingers stroked his skin, and the cat slowly calmed until the growling turned into a soft, rumbling purr. "Maybe later. Right now you need to finish getting healthy." The aroma of her sorrow tainted the air. "I almost lost you. I just found you and I almost lost you, Braden."

"Shhh..." He forgot his need for retribution beneath the weight of her pain. "I'm right here. I'm harder to kill than some human with a knife."

"A poisoned knife."

Fucking pussy human. "A poisoned knife. I'm not going to die on you." He nuzzled the top of her head. "We have to finish our mating, huh?"

Veronica sniffled. "You... when you were..." Her grip on him tightened. "In the forest, you said your tiger wanted me to pull its tail."

He closed his eyes, remembering his tiger's overwhelming craving to have her pounce on them, to tug their tail and solidify their mating. Their souls would connect, and the final connection would snap into place.

Did his tiger still feel that way?

Yes, it purred. It purred, snarled, and growled, making sure he understood its deepest desire. She was a strong female, a stronger wolf, and would make the perfect mother for their cubs and pups. Hell, the cat even accepted the fact their children might howl instead of purr.

"He—we—still do. More than anything. It wants to climb on the altar and complete our mating."

"Yeah?" Her smile blinded him with its intensity, the scent of her pure joy washing over him in a wave of sweetness that had his tiger purring in pleasure. She was what he wanted until the end of time.

"Yeah," he murmured. "But first…" First he had to carve up a particular human. "First, I need to talk to Ares."

CHAPTER TWENTY

Anticipation thrummed in Ronnie's veins. Once Braden woke, he'd quickly regained his strength. A few rare steaks, another nibble at her wrist, and then he was upright. Upright and striding through the house in a loose pair of shorts and nothing else. He would have left the room naked. His focus was on getting to the meeting between Ares, Walter, and the DoPE agents.

"DoPE had nothing to do with tonight's events," Cadman's voice was smooth.

They came around the corner and she quickly surveyed the room, noting the agents stationed throughout the space as well as the handful of sentinels that created a half-circle behind the two alphas. She opened her senses, searching for others that might linger and discovered tigers and wolves were positioned in other places too. The alphas went to the meeting with a small group, but that didn't mean those were the only males ready to defend their leaders.

"Rest assured, we'll put the agency's resources at your disposal." He shook his head. "That Peter would—"

"Who?" She drew everyone's attention, but she only had eyes for Cadman.

"Braden's attacker."

She preferred simply calling him *the human*.

"He said he heard you howl just before he attacked. That he would interfere with a mating…" He feigned surprise as he focused on her father. "She howled for him. That means they weren't mated when your group assaulted those humans." He gave a sad sigh as if he regretted his next words as he turned to Ares. "I'm afraid we're going to have to discuss those events again. If they weren't mated at the time, then your males made an unprovoked attack on those men."

"Cadman," she murmured, stepping away from her mate as anger and rage took over.

The human turned his attention to her, a smile splitting his lips. "Ronnie. I'm happy to see you're unharmed."

She let the wolf come forward, allowed the animal's anger about recent events take over and stretch to fill her human skin. The she-bitch slunk into every inch of her, from nose to toes. She didn't stop until she stood mere inches from him, the male still seated. The beast slipped fur through her pores and lengthened her fangs, ensuring she looked as deadly as the emotions consuming her.

She leaned down, moving slowly, and placed her hands on the arms of the chair. Cadman eased away from her, sitting back the closer she came until the furniture didn't allow him to go any farther. Her prey was caught. "Cadman."

"Uh, Ronnie, I—"

"I'm going to say this once and you're going to listen. Do you understand?" The wolf would only give one warning. She'd been attacked on the side of the road, been subject to this male trying to lock up her mate, and then someone nearly killed him. The animal had been pushed far enough, and if he kept going…

Well, he'd started this fight.

She'd end it.

Permanently.

No one moved or breathed. The DoPE agents tensed at her approach, but even they froze.

"Ronnie—"

"Braden was my mate the second I caught his scent. He was mine the first time I heard his voice. The first time we touched. Mine the first time we kissed." The scent of Cadman's fear teased her wolf and she kept the reins tight. "He was mine when he stopped me from being kidnapped. You want to put a human label on it?"

"You can't intimidate me. I'm—"

Ronnie grinned. "I already am. But you didn't answer my question. Do you want a human label for your reports? You always bitch about them, remember? The paperwork and pencil pushing? I have one for you." She bared her teeth, showing off her fangs. "Mine."

"Ronnie," her father murmured, the warning and request lingering in his tone.

Ronnie, back off.

Ronnie, you can't kill him.

Ronnie, Ares would be pissed if you got blood on the carpet.

Nah, that last one would be Zoe's, and she could practically hear her best friend in her head.

With a huff, she pushed upright but remained in place, staring down at the human. "I'm gonna be the bitch the alphas can't be. They have to play well with others for the good of pride and pack. I'm just a lone female who's gonna recap for you, Cadman. You found out about tigers, and they declared themselves to DoPE. Five DoPE agents then tried to kidnap Claire. Four died, and one of your men succeeded in claiming her."

"They were rogue—"

"I'm not finished," she snapped. "DoPE agents broke into my home at the Lakes and shot me with a wolfsbane dart—"

"They couldn't have been mine. We would never—"

"Their exact words were: *General wants her howling for someone before the end of the week*." She glared at Cadman. "What's your rank now? General, right?"

"It's a title many men carry, and not just those in the United States. I'm sure there are—"

"And then I landed at the Den and three men come after me. Two died. One lived and was sent to the local trauma center. You showed up trying to take us in any way you could." She curled her lip. "What would have happened to me behind bars, Cadman? What would have happened to Braden, Murphy, and Gannon?"

This time the male stayed silent. Ronnie was on a roll. "And then the human—the one who barely clung to life when he left the Den—shows up with a poisoned blade. He looked damned good for a man who was supposedly in ICU. Came here talking about someone giving him a shot, that he'd be strong like a shifter." She sneered. "You can pretend all you want, but we *know* you're involved in this."

"You have no proof."

God, practically an admission of guilt. "I know. My wolf knows. We're not idiots just because we share our bodies with beasts. We'll play well with others—with DoPE—because we have to, but don't for one second think I trust you."

Cadman snorted. "You think your opinion is so important? That you speak for pack and pride?"

She smiled widely, showing off all of her teeth. "Of course not. I'm just a wolf living in a pride, after all. I'm no one, as far as the leadership is concerned. I can say what I want and suffer no consequences. I can say you're a dirty asshole, but I'm just one voice.

"Except, as the mate to the national tiger second, and daughter of the wolf national alpha, I can speak into important ears. They may behave well with others right now, but it doesn't mean they always will. *If* you're involved in our recent troubles—*if*—I recommend you rethink your strategies. You're lazy, it's too messy, and you're going to make an indisputable mistake. You should just give up."

"Or?"

"I shouldn't have to explain shifter justice."

He narrowed his eyes and pushed to his feet. "Is that a threat?"

Ronnie remained in place. She wouldn't be intimidated by a human. "No, simply a reminder."

Suddenly the scent of Cadman's rage exploded from him, the aroma bowling over her like a tsunami, and she realized he'd kept a tight lid on his emotions until that moment. But her words had broken that control.

He was afraid of shifter justice.

He should be.

Evil eyes bored into hers. "I think we're done here. Alphas, we expect a report on the prisoner by morning."

"He'll be dead," her voice was flat.

"Are you suddenly a doctor?"

Ronnie shook her head. "No, but I know he'll answer our questions and then succumb to his injuries, so don't hold your breath. You might want to get his death certificate prepped. It'll save you time later."

Fury suffused his features, those eyes remaining locked onto hers for one second, then five, then... And then he dropped his attention to the floor. It wasn't only wolves who couldn't meet a dominant wolf's stare.

Yes, he glared at the ground, but the stench of his rage whipped toward her and then disappeared as quickly as it arrived. Cadman was pissed but trying to hide it.

"This hostility is unnecessary, Ronnie." The man pressed a hand to the center of his chest. "I swear on my office that DoPE had nothing to do with recent events and we're working hard to discover those responsible for the attacks and the unlawful injection of shifter blood into the human."

New tension thrummed through the room, every shifter stilling as Cadman's words sunk in. Ronnie spoke first, her voice deadly calm. "Injection of shifter blood? Is that what you did?"

Cadman pressed his lips together until they formed a white slash across his face and another whip of anger tinged with panic smacked her. "We'll see ourselves out."

Cadman didn't wait for a response and simply shuffled sideways until he was clear of her body. Then he strode to the front of the house. The DoPE entourage filed out of the room, the last male quietly closing the door behind him. Silence reigned for a moment until Braden spoke.

"That was fucking hot as hell. Made my dick hard."

Ronnie huffed and spun, hands propped on her hips. "Really? I mean, really? With my dad right there, and my mom in the other room?"

He just grinned and shrugged. "Can't help it, baby. You getting up in that human's face…"

"Was stupid." Ares's voice was flat, and she glared at the alpha. "But fucking beautiful and gave us a lot more information about what DoPE has been up to. We'll use that knowledge to dig deeper. Find out more."

"That's my girl. Always cutting through the bullshit." Walter clapped Ares on the shoulder. "She's amazing to take to negotiations. She gets to call bullshit without getting into trouble because she's got enough rank to be there, but not enough to talk on anyone's behalf. You need to cut through all the smoke screens? You take my baby girl."

"No one's taking her anywhere without me," Braden snarled, silencing the chuckles the men shared.

"Well, now, Ares can give orders, and you can't really argue since you're not her mate." Walter's voice was matter-of-fact.

A rumble tore from her mate's throat, the growl stretching through the room, and her wolf reacted to her mate's anger and frustration, jumping forward and wanting to defend him. "We are mates. He made me howl. I'm sure the whole mountain heard."

"Uh-huh." Her daddy looked to her. "But did you pull his tail?"

CHAPTER TWENTY-ONE

Did she pull his tail?

Did she pull his tail?

The answer was no, and it pissed off Braden's tiger. They may not have finished their mating in the forest, but they sure as hell would now. He'd tried to drag her into the woods yesterday so they could fully mate, but she'd denied him. She wanted Braden as healthy as possible. She wasn't going to have people say she didn't deserve him, that she only caught his tail because he was injured.

So he waited, grumbling and growling but content because she'd stayed at his side all day.

Well, it'd been forty-eight hours since he was injured. Forty-eight hours of recovery and taking it easy.

It was time.

Or soon, at least. With a sigh, Braden leaned against the railing at the base of the stairs, half listening to the low murmurs from the women upstairs. Ares came down moments later, but the ladies were still rushing around on the second floor.

He met his friend's gaze. "Are they almost done?"

Ares shrugged. "Apparently this is some rite of passage. I have no fucking clue. They just kicked me out."

He ran a hand through his hair—nerves making him tremble. This would be it, their one and only shot, and they were both ready to put their faith in their animals. He just hoped it wasn't misplaced.

The tiger assured him it wasn't.

Well, they'd see.

"It's not like a human marriage," he mumbled. "She doesn't have to put fucking goop on her face and curl her hair or anything."

The alpha shrugged again. "Yeah, well… women."

Braden growled, his annoyance growing by the second. Sunset had long since passed and he was still waiting for Veronica. "Dammit," he rumbled and tilted his head back, raising his voice so he could be heard. "Dammit, Veronica. We're gonna be fucking naked. How can it take this long to get ready?"

He just wanted to be mated. That was all. His tiger rumbled its agreement. They were over this additional delay. Naked. Shift. Pull. Fuck. That'd been the original plan.

Well, they'd talked about it—a lot—first but then naked. Shift. Pull. Fuck.

Nowhere in there was "wait for hours so she could put on eyeliner perfectly while putting long ringlets in her hair."

What the fuck were ringlets?

"Are you kidding me? You're kidding, right?" Veronica stomped into view and glared at him. "I'm trying to look pretty. I only get mated once in my life and—"

He didn't let her continue. His cat was already at the surface and happy to help him leap up the stairs in two jumps. Then he had her in his arms, plump curves lined up with his hard body, and he reveled in the feel of her against him.

"Baby…" She struggled and the scent of her anger burned his nose. "I just wanna mate you. I don't give a fuck about any of this. I care about you and me in that clearing, shifted and clashing while you try to grab my tail. None of this matters. Just you and me." He pressed his forehead against hers and rubbed their noses together. "I just wanna mate you, baby. Just you."

He knew the very second she gave in. She slumped forward, letting him take her weight, and he held her even tighter. "I wanna mate you, too."

"So come with me. Now. No curlers and eyeliner. No more fussing. No more trying to make it perfect. You're gonna be there. That means it's already perfect." He pressed a soft kiss to her forehead and prayed she'd give in. He knew her mother wanted to make things special, but as long as they were both present, it was already special.

Veronica reached down and twined her fingers with his, and she dropped her voice to a whisper. "Okay, but we have to make a run for it. She'll never—"

"Ronnie? Where did you get off to? We still have to—"

Braden tightened his hold on her hand and spun, dragging her after him. "Run!"

Her tinkling laughter chased them down the hallway, her mother's shout and Zoe's cackle reaching them as they took one turn and the next. He slowed when they approached one of the guest rooms at the end of the hall.

"How far can you jump?" He whipped his shirt over his head and glanced back at her. "You okay with a ten-foot drop?"

"The question is," she released him and dropped her robe, revealing that she was nude underneath. "Can you keep up, pussy?"

She giggled again, running past him and into the room. With a growl, he followed her, tugging and pushing on his jeans until he was nude as well.

Veronica threw the balcony doors open and glanced back at him. "C'mon, kitty."

With that, her change washed over her, a full body shudder that took hardly more than a second. The speed attested to her power and control while her size told him of her strength. She was still smaller than him in shifted form, but she was close to the size of a tigress.

She glanced at him over her shoulder, gray tail wagging and tongue lolling as if to ask him to come play with her. Then she was gone, racing to the edge of the porch and she vaulted over the railing in one leap.

"Fuck," he cursed and let his own change rush forward, the cat's excitement making the transition even quicker than normal.

The second he landed on four paws, he jumped into action, leaping off the railing and flying through the air. He landed on the grass with a low grunt and immediately sought her scent. The animal was ready for a hunt, ready for the chase and the battle that would end with them fully mated.

Veronica switched directions the second she hit the forest, her trail veering right for twenty feet before snapping left and going deeper once more. She wasn't quiet as she ran, wasn't trying to hide her movements. No, it was a rapid race past trees and over bushes, his mate fighting to put space between them. Which… wasn't how this was supposed to happen. They were supposed to head to the altar and fight atop the age-old stone.

But I'm not mating a tiger. I'm mating a wolf.

And when he questioned his tiger, the animal told him to get the fuck over it. This shit was happening *tonight*.

Which meant he dug deep and sought more speed from his inner cat. The feline was happy to supply what he needed. He darted around trees in their path, leaping over larger boulders and digging his claws into the earth when he slipped on leaves. The moon's light was obscured by the forest canopy, making it difficult to see even with his enhanced vision. It didn't matter. He had her scent. He could follow…

Braden slid to a stop beside the creek that ran through pack lands. Had they traveled that far already? Fuck. He was staring at the slowly flowing water, so they obviously had.

He backed away from the shore and narrowed his eyes, searching the bank for proof of her next steps. The tracks ended abruptly at the water's edge, which meant she'd entered, but where did she exit? He looked at the opposite side, hunting for paw marks and saw… none.

What the hell? Dammit, she was making him work for this.

He tilted his head back, scenting the air, but the wind was at his back, pushing her aroma farther away instead of bringing it close. Fuck. He wasn't sure if he should go right or left, and his tiger snarled at him. The human mind had one job.

One. Job.

He growled low, frustrated and furious he'd lost her. How could he claim her if—

A massive body slammed into him, sending him rolling to the left. He allowed the momentum to carry him until he popped to his feet. He crouched low and faced his attacker, a snarl on his lips. He met his opponent's amber-eyed gaze as she matched his rumbling growl.

Veronica had got the drop on him, but now the tiger was engaged, the animal wavering between the desire to have its tail pulled and the need for his mate to prove herself strong and quick enough to claim him.

He narrowed his eyes, scanning her and hunting for any vulnerabilities, and he saw her do the same. They both tensed, bodies ready to collide.

Braden circled left, and Veronica countered the move so they remained opposite each other. The cat already saw her as a cunning foe, but now she had to prove herself to be physically strong as well. It wouldn't mate a weakling.

But she's already endured so much, he whispered to the animal.

She needs to prove herself a little more.

Sometimes he hated the beast.

It assured him the feeling was mutual.

And as he had this conversation with his animal, Veronica made the first move. She took advantage of his distraction and darted forward, teeth nipping his forearm before dancing out of reach once more. He snarled at the sting, shaking his paw as he glared harder. She just gave him a wolfen smile, her tongue lolling. She wasn't upset by his anger in the least.

Braden ignored the cat's instructions and rumblings now, focused entirely on testing his mate. She'd dance forward, and he would jerk out of the way. He would dart into her space, and she would bat him with her massive paw. But she didn't go for the prize.

Didn't she want to mate him? Veronica didn't attempt to capture his tail with her teeth, even when she'd had the opportunity.

Frustration consumed him, anger adding to the mix. If she wasn't going to even *try*…

The tiger took over, snatching control. It was frustrated as well and not just angry but furious. She'd claimed him like a wolf but wasn't willing to mate the tiger in the way of the pride?

When she leaped at him, he batted her aside. When she nipped at him, he dashed out of reach. When she snarled her anger, he merely glared at her. Yeah, well, the cat was pissed too, dammit.

They went on like that, her fighting him while he merely danced out of the way. Time passed, the moon rising higher in the sky and still they were unmated. He could see her growing angrier by the second, but he saw something else as the night brightened. Her fur was damp, strands clumping together with the wetness. Was exhaustion setting in? His cat whimpered. They didn't want her collapsing from fatigue. They were so much larger than her, so much stronger. They didn't want their little wolf to pass out from the strain. It was ingrained in him to care for her. Even as she annoyed them. Even if she wasn't strong enough to tug his tail.

He paused in their fight and released a questioning trill, quietly asking her if she was okay as he took a cautious step forward. He'd roar for help if she was too winded. He'd—

Braden saw nothing but a blur of gray race past him before a fierce jolt of pain raced down his spine. He snarled with the sudden ache and snapped his jaws at his attacker—at his mate. Who had her jaw clamped around his tail and laughter in her eyes. He glared harder, and she released him, giving the abused flesh a soft lick and gentle nudge.

His tiger roared with joy as the last of their mating bond snapped into place. The final bindings spun between them, and he felt the first moment when their thoughts collided and their minds connected. Emotions flowed steadily between them, ebbing and flowing, twisting, and turning as their connection solidified.

He sensed her joy, her overwhelming happiness at finally catching him. And smug. She was damned smug.

He twitched his tail away from her. *"That hurt."*

"And I'm tired, but I still got you. You're mine now."

"It took you long enough," he grumbled.

"When you can't win through strength, win through cunning."

"You're saying you're smarter than me." He curled his lip and bared a single fang.

"I'm not saying I'm smarter than you, baby. I'm simply saying one of us failed here, and it wasn't me."

Braden turned and padded closer, nuzzling her scruff. *"Pain in the ass."*

"Good thing I love you, then. And you love me."

Yeah, he did. More than she could ever imagine. *"Yes, and I can't wait to show you I love you again and again."*

"Race you back to the house?"

Braden didn't spare a moment to respond. Instead, he spun and delved back into the forest. He had a mate to fuck and babies to create.

"Babies?" Veronica screeched within his mind.

"Babies. Lots of babies."

"But what about all the drama with…"

Braden slid to a stop and spun to face her. *"There will always be drama, there will always be threats to the pride, and there will always be things that try and stand in our way, but baby… I'll always love you, I'll always protect you, and I'll always kick anyone's ass who tries to stand between us and what we want."* He strode toward her and licked her muzzle. *"Always."*

When she didn't say a word, he stepped back and was gratified when she moved toward him and stopped at his side.

Of course, that's when Violet came storming through the brush, tongue lolling out and eyes dancing. She barked and lowered her front, ass sticking up and tail wagging.

"Are you kidding? Am I about to get cock-blocked by your sister?"

"You did say you wouldn't let anyone stand in our way…"

He looked at her from the corner of his eye. *"Can you jump over her? Outrun her?"*

Veronica snorted. *"Try and keep up."*

By the tone of her voice, he had a feeling he'd spend his life trying to keep up with her and he… looked forward to it.

THE END

purchasing decisions. So, go forth and rate my level-o-awesome!

The Tiger Tails series:
Fast and the Furriest
You're Kitten Me

About the Author

Ex-dance teacher, former accountant and erstwhile collectible doll salesperson, New York Times and USA Today bestselling author Celia Kyle now writes paranormal romances for readers who:

1) Like super hunky heroes (they generally get furry)
2) Dig beautiful women (who have a few more curves than the average lady)
3) Love laughing in (and out of) bed.

It goes without saying that there's always a happily-ever-after for her characters, even if there are a few road bumps along the way.

Today she lives in Central Florida and writes full-time with the support of her loving husband and two finicky cats.

If you'd like to be notified of new releases, special sales, and get FREE eBooks, subscribe here: http://celiakyle.com/news

You can find Celia online at:
http://celiakyle.com
http://facebook.com/authorceliakyle
http://twitter.com/celiakyle

COPYRIGHT PAGE

Manufactured by Amazon.ca
Bolton, ON

24609436R00113